Measure
of
Reality

The
Measure
of
Reality

The Measure of Reality

Maija
Timonen

Book Works

Table of Contents

The Frozen Father

Spring was here. Her efforts to keep the lid of the chest freezer closed had failed, and she was now sitting sideways on top of the thawing father, gripping his wrists tightly, pressing down his arms, which were crossed over his chest.

As he was still partially frozen, the scope of his facial movement was limited, but the little there was he reserved for a sneering half-grin, mocking her futile attempts to keep him down. With each insidious ray of sun a tiny bit more of him was jarred loose. He released the occasional contemptuous snort as she tried to get the attention of people walking by, who were seemingly oblivious to her existence.

She tried to scream at them to come help her, tell them that he was going to get away, but no sound would come out of her mouth, her hoarse wordless wheezing echoing the way the specific content of his alleged crimes too was beyond her abilities to articulate, even to herself. She could not pin down the details of his infractions any more than she could hold down his large defrosting carcass, about to break free.

Romcom

I sometimes think about films I would make if I had the means and professional standing to support such ambitions.

A serial synopsiser, I like coming up with evocative outlines for stories, cryptically meaningful sketches with much of the detail missing. My most recent project(ion) is about an artist woman who develops an 'ironic' obsession with a famous actor.

> *The name of the actor should always be bleeped out when mentioned.*

The artist is not successful in her career, she is single, in her late thirties, and her bad experiences with romance have led her to be entirely alienated from sexual relationships. Her celebrity crush is in fact an extension of the way the prospect of any kind of romantic relationship has become completely unreal to her. The prospect of having a relationship with a celebrity is as fantastical to her as that of having a relationship with any of the people she meets on a daily basis, and in seeming equally unattainable, they become interchangeable.

> *She is shown growing increasingly unsexy and asexual in every social situation she enters into.*

She attempts to fill the sexual gap in her life by fantasising about the actor, but even in her fantasies cannot escape her deep sense of emptiness and the feeling that all that she has strived for in her life, her 'work', amounts to nothing. She imagines a chance encounter between herself and the celebrity, but hard as she tries, the scene always unravels at the point where he asks her what she does for a living.

> *This nonstarter fantasy is repeated again and again toward the beginning of the film with varying alternative progressions – one in which she looks pained when asked, one in which she is seen talking, but nothing can be heard. He also has different responses: laughing, looking a little confused as if rejected, walking away with a slightly incredulous look on his face.*

> *Her silence becomes the void toward which everything else that happens in the film gravitates.*

The persistence of the inarticulation, the inability to say what you do for a living, seemed somehow connected – beyond mere analogy – to an inability to bridge the gap between one's sexual feelings and words that might express them, or even the opportunity or occasion for their actualisation.

> *The problem was both chronic and acute – her formative fantasy, the one caught in a loop, resided in this gap where nothing could come out of her mouth. Or into it.*

Fantasies and dreams are a way of accessing hidden dimensions of everyday experience, but what happens when you can't fantasise? The constant feeling that she had, of the real state of things being obscured from her, that there was some underlying truth that others had access to but she didn't, was surely something to do with this inability of hers, her stuckness – 'reality' kept fading out of her reach, out of her view, as she careered further into the self-defeating vacuum.

The woman eventually tells of this inability to consummate her fantasy to a friend. She outlines her problem as the inability to explain, even to herself, what she does for a living. That even a simple fantasy fades out into a rambling sea of nebulous evasion. Her friend offers a simple solution to the problem: a one-line answer to the dreaded work question from her and a one-line comeback from the actor. With these words the scenario is released from the deadlock and allowed to move on.

'I am an artist. I make weird films.'

'Are they are as charming as you? I love them already.'

In the banality of these lines the woman sees a way out of her dilemma: Cut through the elaboration. Change context. Move from art to the realm of generic models of fiction, the ready-made narratives that she had previously viewed with contempt.

She decides that she has overreached in her efforts to convince the world of her competence; in fact less effort was needed, at least the effort needed to be directed differently, into outward action, not into the construction of ever more complex thought-models by which to translate her experience into art.

Models that would inevitably just act as agents of deferral, as forces that cast her deeper into her own head as opposed to being something that might help her climb out of there.

The answer was staring her in the face: she would make a romantic comedy and with this transform her life. In keeping with her newfound commitment to simplifying things, she recalls scriptwriting advice about allowing for only one verb – 'to say' – as a means of carrying dialogue forward. As in:

The Measure of Reality

'I have spent a lot of time thinking about our future together',
the artist said.

'Now you can stop thinking about it and start living it!'
said the actor.

> *At this point the film jumps ahead in time. It is not quite known*
> *how we get here, but against all odds the woman has ventured*
> *into the world of commercial filmmaking, and has cast the*
> *object of her obsession in her debut film. A romantic interlude*
> *ensues between the woman and the actor, a seemingly*
> *exceptional coming together of two people. Genuine closeness*
> *can be read into their gestures, which are shot close up and*
> *performed by the players with the kind of relaxed subtlety that*
> *always makes one wonder if they weren't having a relationship*
> *off camera too.*

> *And then...*

> *Nothing.*

What for a moment seemed so real is suddenly like it never
happened. The mystery of love has not opened itself up to
the woman after all – it remains a fantasy, even after its
realisation. We backtrack and recap:

> *There is no such thing as just a fantasy. The inarticulable*
> *experiences that speak through the fantasy need to be taken*
> *as having historical value, and fantasy itself is not a projection*

Romcom

forward, as it might appear to be, but a backward projection, the light we cast on past events to make sense of an inexplicable present.

It is suggested that *'her formative fantasy, the one caught in a loop'* is about more than just the inability to speak out. Maybe it was the relationship between the improbable coming true, and a humiliation involved in it being swiftly snapped away, that constituted the artist's primal scene of sorts. Perhaps that was the traumatic thing that made up the stuff of her fantasies.

The woman had one story in particular that occupied this place for her, and allowed her to make sense of the painful sense of rejection that had surrounded her throughout the years – as well as perhaps playing some role in predetermining the outcome of any new situation she found herself in. The story concerned her first kiss, and whatever was the true order of events, the real nuance and detail, this was how she told it:

At the age of fourteen, she had had a crush on a boy a slightly older friend was at school with. He was very handsome but sweet-looking (slightly cross-eyed so as to not be too obviously beautiful), good at everything, from writing to playing the guitar, and his mother was a glamorous author. Younger and not particularly socially forward, the girl could not imagine her infatuation becoming anything more than that. One Friday evening at a party, in the early 1990s, without any forewarning or prelude, he came over, sat on the girl's lap and kissed her. Then, he stood up and walked away. This did not bother her as it was perfectly in keeping with what passed for the norm in awkward sexual interactions between teenagers. The following week, her friend approached the boy in school, and confronted him about the kiss, presumably under the guise of being protective of the younger girl. Perhaps slightly afraid of having caused offence, he defended himself and said: 'I'm sorry. I was so drunk I thought your friend was someone else, the girl I came to the party with. They look very similar.'

Instead of keeping the details of this faux pas to herself, for reasons best known only to her, the girl's friend divulged them, sowing the seeds of a future revolving around a fixation. One in which the realisation of a sexual fantasy inevitably performs the voiding of its basis in reality. So much could, of course, be said of anyone, but seasoning this fixation, adding that extra something to its problematic nature, was the setting in of a belief that all women are interchangeable with each other in the eyes of men, at least inasmuch as they fall close to each other on the axis on which women's physical characteristics are recorded and gauged.

Now looking at the reshuffled components of this constellation of disappointments, it occurred to her that it might not have been so much that her inability to imagine herself into the romantic scenario with the actor constituted an inability to fantasise, but rather that the only fantasy available to her entailed rejection, an unhappy outcome.

If trauma is indeed secondary to the fantasies it produces, as Freud claimed, her rejection-fantasy had long since become a sign of something reaching far beyond it – and herself. ◊ Banal encounters and moments folded back into that single incident all those years ago (had it even taken place?), creating a network of correspondences. The revelations unravelling at these intersections projected both inwards and outwards, the unconscious dredged up being both her own and of the world she lived in. What it spoke of was an erasure of a myriad of subjective experiences – a hollow history.

Everywhere she looked, she saw herself absent. She also saw the holes where others should have been. There was some limited hopefulness to this pockmarked view of the world. Having a fantasy of absence was preferable to an absence of fantasy (a concern I had had before). Propelled by these epiphanies, the fantasy made itself known with increased frequency, giving an expression to the traumatic nature of the reality she lived in.

Note: ◊ Freud implied in his *Wolf Man* case study that trauma can be perceived or articulated in the meeting of selected points in time, of apparently unrelated events that otherwise might have been innocuous. A seemingly banal scenario can appear horrific in a nightmare; trauma has its own temporality that bends time. In describing the differences between French psychoanalysis, American ego psychology and British object relations theory, Juliet Mitchell summarises the French take as leaning heavily on Freud's idea of *Nachträglichkeit* ('afterwardness'), the retroactive attribution of meaning to childhood events, real or imagined. She seems to describe its curious temporality as a kind of continual present that dwells in a non-existent history: 'There is nothing, no event, experience, feeling, to remember, there is only a past whose meaning is realised in the present.' Juliet Mitchell, *Mad Men and Medusas: Reclaiming Hysteria*, (Basic Books, 2001), p. 284.

This dynamic seemed particularly pertinent to the protagonist's predicament – she could see that the factual details of past slights and disappointments did not matter, that it did not matter if they were real or not, their significance was only for the present and the present was the only proof they required to be taken seriously. They were only the fantastical facilitators of further fantasies that brought the present moment into focus, with all its flaws and contradictions. But while expressing something important about absence, a past whose historical value

  The Measure of Reality

was only to the present was also troubling. This absence of history plagued her, erased her, produced an impasse where she could not see herself becoming anything beyond the absence itself. Without a past there was surely not to be a future either. The eternal present was not simply a timeless time. Evidence was mounting: it was in fact also the end of time.

The Sniffers

There it was:

> '... *predominance of sex detached from emotions implies much greater difficulty in the interpretation of each sexual protagonist's actual feelings and intentions.*' ◊

The first thing going through her head was 'You don't say?', but of course it wasn't said, it was written, and it seemed that, surprisingly enough, much could be gotten away with in written form. The weak links in arguments, the points from *a* to *c* that did not quite mount up to a *b*, sentences that carried the text forward, but which their writer secretly hoped would slip past without too much scrutiny – well, they quite often did.

Not here though. There was definitely something missing. There was an unqualified assumption that sex detached from emotions was indeed somehow predominant. In what way? Where? For whom?

Maybe in 'popular representations'?

That didn't seem right either. Surely the most oppressive ideology floating around was romance. The harmonious co-existence of independent but publicly associated conceptions of sex and love. Like a sort of a glorious show-marriage, the cold power couple in the business of sexuality, romance had nothing to do with the actually occurring causal relation and inseparable unity of sex and love, but it purported to uphold a connection between the two.

The Measure of Reality

She also thought:

> *'Am I a sexual protagonist? The heroine of my own erotic novel?'*

She imagined herself as the emotionally indecipherable consumer of sport-like sex, but it seemed somehow thin and improbable, out of kilter with the psychosomatic complexities of the oppressive forces acutely bearing down on her sense of sexual expression.

Sure, sex detached from emotions sounded bad, but what was really amiss with this idea, to her, was that she hadn't considered it even to be possible. People who bragged about the depths of their alienation (and these people did exist), insisting that they were able to section off their sexual activities from their everyday operations, struck her as misguided fools who'd bought into the lie that they could be the masterful auteurs of their own sex lives. Sex is social, and even if to them this separation would have appeared real, it always arose and existed in relation to someone else, through activity done *with* someone else, a someone else whose feelings and emotional responses they had no control over. Where people claimed to be able to separate sex and feelings (or sex and life), it did not strike her as an actual separation, but rather a repression of a connection. What made the situation worse was that the complex webs of relations and feelings they were repressing did not simply pertain to their own psychosexual makeup. They were forcibly trying to repress those of other people.

And what is repressed has a tendency to return.

> *'... predominance of sex detached from emotions implies much greater difficulty in the interpretation of each sexual protagonist's actual feelings and intentions.'*

There might not always be feelings of affection that went with sex, but there were always feelings – be they confusion, disgust, annoyance, doubt, disappointment, boredom, pity. It was exactly the individual's tendency to form cathexes of whatever nature to the act and idea of sex that made it such a prominent site of exploitation.

In distinction to this, the hypothetical sex-without-emotions exists for nothing but itself: like a hermetic commodity deprived of the dynamic and social nature of capitalism it is not really consumable, not really even desirable, it is only a distant reminder of the imperative to desire desire. It is sex as a marker of an abandoned duty to feel in the correct way, a duty that we can't possibly live up to, not in the sense 'sex' (the idea invested with agency) seems to oblige. The feelings and intentions hidden behind our sexual behaviours aren't exactly hidden, they are just pretty irrelevant to the feelings we are supposed to have.

Maybe this was what the *'sex detached from emotions'* was referring to, the predominance of sex the affective dimension of which was ignored and suppressed in favour of a formal, contractual even, association with a purely ideal version of feelings...

'... *predominance of sex detached from emotions implies much greater difficulty in the interpretation of each sexual protagonist's actual feelings and intentions.'*

It was all so complicated and confusing. She knew something was not right with the statement, but the more she tried to unpack it, the more concepts clung to each other, lay heavy on top of each other, slid into one another forming a congealed orgiastic mass, obstinate in the face of her powers of reasoning that were trying to wedge its constituents apart. All that she managed to do was find herself with the occasional sweaty cold lump of thought left in her reluctant hand, emitting a dubious odour of post-rationality. Thought that seemed vacant and self-satisfied having reached its goal, no longer concerned with much of anything beyond its state of (merely adequate) completion.

(Maybe what was meant was not sex detached from emotions, but a conflict between sexual desires and romantic aspirations?)

But she thought further, thinking that despite all evidence pointing toward the interlinkedness of all things, toward the undeniable physicality of all thought and all emotion, the in-separability of sex and emotion, there was also something undeniable about the contested statement too. Things that sound like truisms do so because most of the time they are true in one way or another. *'Predominance of sex detached from emotions'* was perhaps true because despite initial appearances, underneath it all the statement was not about consumerism, about consuming 'sex' the commodity in an alienated fashion, but about its exact opposite. It belied not only the impossi-bility of consumption, the scarcity of goods to consume, but also the absence of the libidinal dimension of consumption, the absence of desire. The instrumentalisation of desire had somehow, without anyone noticing, turned into its slow fading away.

And this was a current sort of problem, with many proposed solutions.

Six out of ten users of internet dating services such as Guardian Soulmates complain about the absence of 'spark' in their dates.

'We hear this more and more all the time. It is hard to conjure feeling for someone you really don't know that much about. You can control the process by making sure the date meets a certain set of criteria before you meet them, but this can only go so far.

The Sniffers

*The 'chemistry', if you will, is missing. This is what we are
trying to address, we are trying to put the excitement back into
dating.'* ◊

Jane, 28, puts it more bluntly:
    *'It's such a time-waster. You meet someone online, they tick
the right boxes, you exchange messages for a couple of weeks
before meeting. But then when you do, they smell awful. You
really know from the first moment. Unless of course they are
wearing a strong aftershave, which can lead to wasting even
more time.'*

The article described a new dating innovation, requiring
that participants brought with them a T-shirt they had
worn for some time, which would be placed on a table with
others. Prospective dates could then smell said shirts. If anyone liked the smell of a particular T-shirt, they had the option
of meeting the person it belonged to (she could imagine
the mawkish and largely gestural camaraderie forming
between the people attending these events, the shared
giggles over the silliness of sniffing T-shirts acting as a
bonding agent that occasionally produced a lucky extra-
pheromonal match).

The picture illustrating the article was of a woman
with blond hair pressing her face against a piece of fabric,
presumably one of the T-shirts. The image was ambiguous.
Rather than smelling it, it looked more as if she was crying,
burying her face into it to cover her tears. It looked as if she
was in the grips of the initial shock of losing a loved one and
wanted to be submerged in the last item still bearing the proof
of their physical existence as if this could defer the tragedy
that had already taken place. It seemed that in one knee-jerk
swing from the pure numbers of internet dating, the boxes
ticked for compatibility and preferred qualities, to the pure

The Measure of Reality

biology of pheromones, the T-shirt sniffers had captured something about how lost we all were.

It nevertheless struck her that there was no allowance made for how our desires come into being socially, in the course of our psychic development from infancy to adulthood (we want what we see others wanting, we want others to approve of us, therefore we instinctively align our desires with theirs – or so the theory went in any case). ◊ By skipping over this complex social composition of desire, the sniffers had simultaneously done away with what was truly individual about us and our sexual longings (through which the indignant remnants of our sense of self were most furiously asserted), as well as drawing a veil over the ways in which this individuality was a plant, the source of a profound sense of alienation. ◊

It was only occasionally and for fleeting moments that this paradox was graspable by reason, but the tornness at its centre made itself known whenever any desire was felt. Having a crush on someone for her always entailed a sense of expansion. She thought whether or not something could or would happen between her and the object of her desire, this feeling, of really being the person she was, but more – of being more herself – by virtue of her desire, could not be taken away from her. Yet, as painful as it was, she could also see that whoever she fixed her sights on, they were always also found attractive by scores of other people too. That what she was feeling, the thing that seemed so irrefutably hers, to the extent of being her, was also on some level what she was 'supposed' to feel or be. That the very sense of being somebody was hinged on not really being anybody in particular after all.

And now, she thought, with their crude understanding of sexual attraction, which focused on the biological at the price of the social, the sniffers were trying to kill off even our perceived right to take pleasure in our pain – or pain in our pleasure.

'But aren't feelings a little more complex than just biology?'
'No! In any case, you can't sustain a relationship with someone who smells awful, you just can't!'

This seemed to her to be more a process of exclusion rather than one of selection. Weed out the ones you know you truly would not be able to stand, and then just hope that one of the others will take you; ensuring that being 'physically intimate' with them won't make you want to hurl. In the beginning in any case.

The T-shirt sniffers' misunderstanding about the site and composition of desire, however implicated in the workings of capitalism this desire was, was still a privileged position, but one foreboding the expansion of not only affective poverty, but of material poverty that slowly ate away at the remnants of our compromised longings. The scarcity that had been defining people's lives elsewhere, was inextricably tied to sexuality, and as wealth drifted out of the reach of those who previously had felt a claim to it, so too did the preconditions for their desiring of desire.

She thought back to a someone she used to know, an American who had lived for years without access to health services. Anxiety about the possibility of getting ill, and no doubt the actuality of getting ill without the option of going to see a doctor, instead having to opt for the hope of getting better without the comfort of knowing what it was, really, that was ailing him, had forged a very particular relationship between the American and his body. A steely, detached, but protective relationship. His body was his suspicious temple, hard yet vulnerable, fortified against obvious damage, but still an open stage for emotional dramas to play out upon. Dramas he attempted to subject to the rule of his idiosyncratic moral laws. Laws that seemed weak and haphazard, suffering from the lack of external support and guidance.

All this gave him the air of physical and emotional meanness that was brought into special relief when sex entered the equation. There, he emitted a chill of pornified clinicality – a reluctant compliance to the imperative to be 'sexy', to engage in sexual acts profusely and without repression, as if they were a sporting feat, a mental and physical challenge. And of course they were. For him perhaps more than most people. His fear of infection merged with his fear of investing his feelings in the wrong object. The challenge was to endure this risk, to swim the channel of sexual union covered in a thick protective layer of grease. There could be no giving or receiving, as the latter meant he might get 'something' – some unnameable disease – and the former meant he might be re-linquishing something invaluable, as if affection were a finite possession one could not get back once one had parted with it. Fear of bacteria became in him inseparable from the fear of being wrong about his choice of partner.

This made her think of 'friendly bacteria'. What were they really trying to evoke when they said this? To her it sounded like just another way of drawing lines where none existed. Our bodies were filled with bacteria, and nominating them as friendly or not seemed to be about inclusion and exclusion, us and them. Friend or enemy. Is it OK to touch your bacteria? It's friendly, right? Her ideology alarms went off once more, and her brain whirred on, jumping from one association to another. Bacteria was all over our skins, all over our world, it was the unseen world, a collective biological unconscious – was 'chemistry' supposed to work with or against this unconscious? She wished she were better informed.

It had not occurred to her then, when she knew the American, that this lack of generosity could spread, eventually becoming the psychosomatic manifestation of a state of economic deprivation on her home turf too. She had shaken her head at it, felt sorry for him and 'people like him', but had ultimately been unaffected by it, cocooned in some sensory smugness brought on by economic privilege. Now the plague was hard to deny. The poverty that had always been there was creeping up and pushing the former middle classes into a defensive position. There was a need to hold onto your own, to ration feeling, to invest it some-where safe (under your mat-tress, perhaps). And of course it was not simply about emotional entrenchment (as if such a thing could be separated from any other kind), but – like with the American sport-of-sex-boy – about protecting yourself against poverty and physical illness, against the virulent nature of desperation.

> *'... predominance of sex detached from emotions implies much greater difficulty in the interpretation of each sexual protagonist's actual feelings and intentions.'*

Asked whether she had ever had a sexual encounter that she thought fit the description 'detached from emotions', either on her part or the part of the person she had the encounter with, the girl interviewed in the paper answered in the affirmative. When pushed for more elaboration on how this had felt, and whether the detachment had made it difficult to decipher the stakes, this is what she had to say:

> *'I guess I did find him completely obtuse. I felt obtuse myself. Some people claim they can partition sex and life – sex and feelings – and perhaps they can, but it occurs to me that this is made possible by separating not "sex" but the person they have sex with from the rest of their lives. The other person becomes the guardian of the label "sex", and as far as their sexual partner is concerned, synonymous with this label. Their humanity, if not erased, is dramatically reduced.'*

> *'Do you think that pheromonal match-making has addressed this issue of unknown motives for you?'*

The Measure of Reality

'Erm... No I don't think so. I am not sure any one thing could. I have been in situations, both pheromonally and non-pheromonally initiated, where I really thought we had something. I mean that I thought the feelings were mutual, or at least complimentary, and was sure that the situation was going somewhere only for it to end in an unexplained cutting off of communications. You don't ever know what anyone is thinking. So I guess it's not that it's more difficult to see motivations with detached sex, it may be equally difficult or perhaps even a little less misleading as sex accompanied by assurances of commitment. These days, who wants to take risks? Emotional resources are becoming increasingly valuable, and maybe you don't want to squander them on something like sex.' ◊

This chimed with something rather alarming she had once heard said about the relation of poverty and sexuality (the context in which it was said had probably been integral to its intended meaning, but she could not recall it): the poor don't desire sex, they desire prosperity, and in times of desperation sex becomes a means for the acquisition of prosperity – not something to be enjoyed. To this it could now be added that, at times of increasing insecurity, the solace and support found in affective bonds becomes a crucial means of survival. You could not be profligate with your emotional energies anymore. The whims and fancies of sexual attraction were surely too unpredictable to gamble on when the whole infrastructure of your life was at stake. Sex and love divorced and sex lost out in the settlement. And we all moved back in to live with our parents. ◊

Notes: ◊ Eva Illouz, *Why Love Hurts: A Sociological Explanation* (Polity, 2012), p. 46.

◊ Missing 'chemistry', as raised by the sniffing event's organiser, did not really even begin to cover what was wrong with internet dating. Part of the problem was that internet dating services performed a curious sort of literalisation of the metrics that already played some part in informing people's romantic choices. Of the preferred age, interests, tastes, income bracket, it created a new form of sociality that seemed to be like a parody of the one existing in real life. The flexibility that still existed in real-life social interactions, which despite the generally normative and limited nature of people's social spheres allowed for ambiguities and permitted sexual attraction to arise as a singularity – despite not because of these norms – was entirely cut out at the first point of contact online. It was supposedly recovered again if an actual encounter ensued, but the barrier had already been erected, it had already drawn lines around people, and worked to define their choices – established the parameters of their socio-sexual mobility. To give an example of this, if you were a woman of about thirty-eight, who was single and led a fairly sociable life, mixing with people of different ages with similar interests, you might have come to think it a reasonable expectation that you might also date people from a rather broad age range, from their late twenties to their mid-forties, or more to the point, you might not have seen age in itself as such a defining feature of your existence. On an online dating site however, where people assessed each other cautiously, based on broad impressions, expectations and probabilities, age would become something way more definite than it was elsewhere. So if you were a thirty-eight-year-old woman, you could be sure that no man under forty-five would contact you, even if you were open to being contacted by them. If the risk of being rejected by someone you didn't really want in the first place loomed large over every effort at finding a romantic connection, this risk became less a risk, more a probability in the economies of online dating.

The Measure of Reality

◊ What was missing in the sniffers' take could be summarised by the well-known Lacanian dictum, 'Desire is the desire of the Other'. For Lacan 'desire' is a person's desire to be recognised, and part of this is desiring what one believes the Other to desire. This could be understood in many ways, from the kinds of immediate social ties that inform what we find attractive, to being conditioned into broader societal norms of attractiveness. T-shirt sniffing failed to account for any of its innumerable stratifications. It remained firmly on the stale forecourts of feeling where no desire could be stirred, no interest piqued.

◊ The way she saw herself as torn between a sense that her romantic feelings were the most private part of her, the one thing that gave her some integrity as a subject, and an awareness of how thoroughly informed by nauseating popular narratives of what romantic love consisted of these feelings were, could, she hoped, be somehow allevi-ated if placed in a historical context. Eva Illouz sees this paradox as a feature of modernity. She explains this in sociological terms and as part of the changed geography of romantic choice. She argues that in modernity, a 'great transformation' (after Karl Polanyi) occurs where romantic choice is dis-embedded from moral codes, and romantic feeling becomes individualised, that with the dawn of the modern self we come to perceive love as integral to our being rather than something that responds and consciously moulds itself to external conditions; hierarchies and rules of conduct. Through this shift we have become more vulnerable to the vagaries of the romantic marketplace. A shift from the moral dictates of an immediate community to mass-media norms of attractiveness constitutes a simultaneous move inwards and further out of our reach. Sexual feeling becomes part of an essentialised self while the 'social context' conditi-oning desire now refers to an even more impersonal realm. In the transition away from romantic choices being dominated by the interests of the immediate community, the criteria for these choices has become simultaneously more individualised, subjective, 'irrational' if you will, at the same time as it is everywhere conditioned by cultural norms of attractiveness as well as social status – economic motivations become mixed in with vague measurements of 'sexiness'. She writes: 'because there are no more formal mechanisms by which people pair up, individuals internalize the economic dispositions that also help them make choices which must be at once economic and emotional, rational and irrational.' *Why Love Hurts*, p. 53.

Illouz's use of the word internalisation is (maybe) interesting if looked at more closely, and could possibly help unpack this conflict between rational and irrational romantic choice. Freud saw internalisation of (paternal) authority as a necessary stage of development of the individual into a relatively autonomous being. Absorbing the structures of domination into your psyche – the ego representing reason that must act to curb the instinctual drives of the id – is a simultaneous submission and point of resistance to authority. Critical theorists such as Theodor Adorno concurred with this logic, but saw reason and nature (instincts) as existing in an unresolved impasse – civilisation ever underpinned by instinctual drives, thus 'reason' is never reason in a true sense, but rationalisation, instrumental reason – which led to the triumph of authority. For a full account see: Jessica Benjamin, 'The End of Internalisation: Adorno's Social Psychology', *Telos*, 1977, no. 32, pp. 42–64. In fact Illouz's statement could be described as being about the *loss* of internalisation in the Freudian sense – it is not 'internalisation' per se, but could have affinity with an argument put forward by critical theorists and discussed by Jessica Benjamin in the above-mentioned text. This argument, attaching itself to the change in family structures and the rise of consumer culture after WW2, sketched a situation in which the controlling function of the ego had been removed from the equation in the absence of identifiable authority to internalise ('the death of the father'), and in which the dominant forces of capitalism therefore had direct access to our instincts.

The neoliberal appropriation of the freedom-seeking rhetoric of 1960s countercultures, could be said to

The Measure of Reality

manifest in our sex/love lives as an increasingly painful contradiction between the rhetorical imperative to enjoy our individuality (and our mythologically individual sexual makeup), and this individuality being a rhetorical imperative. The more we are told that our desires are our own – to do what we want with – the more they are accessed directly and manipulated by the interests of capital. Or are they? She thought further. To her mind this process of manipulation was so transparent that it surely failed to convince anyone these days; it was more like empty posturing in front of a disinterested, undesiring audience, who despite being disinterested, still mysteriously did what they were told. True compliance, with no real manipulation necessary.

Now that she reflected on various complex claims made about the relation of love and sex (which aligned with a kind of argument about the relation of mind and body, even the relation of the ideal and the material), she began to realise that her insistence on the interconnected-ness of the two, on the hard-to-pin-down dynamism of their connection, was a losing battle. It was away from the banal certainties of each category and in this dynamic relation that desire was allowed to exist, but desire now raised its tormented head with decreasing frequency and she thought this was significant. Most weeks it was nowhere to be felt and all proclamations by others to the contrary, which she saw posted on 'confessional' Twitter feeds, filled her with a sense of smug cunning: *she* saw through their performativities, their efforts to hold onto a receding realm of the senses... Maybe, she thought, this was the role of an unreasonable and inflated ego, the ego still there but in its death throes, about to pop. Maybe, the rationale of this (maniacal) ego, was to convince us of our ability *to* desire rather than to curb and ration desire. The role of the ego now, was maybe to convince you that you weren't, yet, quite, dead inside.

Then there was of course the slightly different second coming of the ego, or of some approximation of the rationality it represented: the rise of ideologies of the family.

◊ In his essay 'Is it Love?' Brian Kuan Wood offers a view on a contemporary crisis situation. He questions the role of love (in general, not merely romantic love) in a world where the private and public spheres have become confused and entwined, and where the decline of public infrastructures casts love and emotional commitment as surrogates for them. A retreat into family and support found in affective bonds threatens to establish a kind of tyranny of the subjective in a world without subjects.

In the changed western economic landscape since the 1970s the rise of individualism combined with increasingly precarious conditions of the 'flexible' labour market effected an ever greater demand of self-management. 'Being your own boss' seems, at least in part, to follow the logic of a nostalgia for that lost rational ego, for the lost 'father'. The self-subjection inherent to 'being your own boss' resembles the internalisation of authority as sketched out by Freud, but with the distinction that the external authority it is sup-posed to negotiate with is rather different. It expects the subject to enslave themselves on behalf of external powers that do not appear in a clear and tangible form (and if they do, their form of appearance is not that of reason but of force): economic imperative (in its neoliberal guise) presents itself as an increasingly absolute yet entirely abstract ruler. What the subject experiences of it within the self-management model then, is perhaps a kind of instinctual barbarity that they are expected to leash upon themselves – a kind of an intensification then of the version of internalisation (the generalisation of paternal authority) put forward by critical theorists. Brian Kuan Wood, 'Is it Love?', *e-flux journal* #53, March 2014.

◊ The reversion back to familial structures of support in the face of declining support from societal bodies and the false autonomy of self-management (a kind of imitation of internalisation) seem somehow joined in their regres-sive nostalgia for the symbolic function of the family. In an article entitled 'Mothers', Jacqueline Rose touches on one of the reasons why this familial pull is so

The Measure of Reality

problematic. She remarks on how while promoting family values and a kind of neoliberal cult of motherhood, the conservative government in the UK are also making it increasingly hard to be a mother through their austerity policies: 'One of the most striking characteristics of discourse on mothering is that the idealisation doesn't let up as reality makes the ideal harder for mothers to meet. If anything, it seems to intensify.' Jacqueline Rose, 'Mothers', *London Review of Books*, 2014, vol. 36, no. 12, pp. 17-22.

The Aftershave

I am trying to remember when I first noticed it. I don't think it was the first time I met him. It was later. Remembering our first encounter as scent-free allowed me for a long time to think there was something 'real' about the whole thing, some undeniable biological attraction even if circumstances dictated it never be acted out. That it was not all just a product of my pathological relationship with barriers. Now I know better, but before I explain about the scent, I want to describe the first time I met him – the unscented time, or the time before my thoughts passed the point of no return.

I remember piling into the backseat of a taxi, which was uncomfortably crowded. Uncomfortable, that is, until I gained a sensory awareness of the entire left side of my body being pressed against his right side. This was not uncomfortable, but instead filled me with excitement. His side was warm and solid, like an unrestrictive hug. I didn't even know him but I wanted to turn and flip my body over his, to maximise surface coverage. He was breathing quite heavily, and though good sense told me this was perhaps to do with the exertion being drunk put on one's body, I still wanted to think it was because he was feeling something similar to me. Later on in the evening our knees accidentally touched under the table, and the touch was held for considerably longer than appropriate. I suspected this was because of a mutual reluctance to make the other person feel embarrassed, not because of a magnetic pull between our bodies, but I chose to believe otherwise.

A lot of time passed before I saw him again, and when I did – I think it was in the street, we were sort of neighbours – he leaned in to kiss me on the cheek. I immediately felt a bit choked by the power of his aftershave or deodorant, whichever it was. It seemed he had put it on just on his way out of the house. I wanted to access the swoony feeling from the cab, but the scent made me cranky. It alerted me to itself, shutting out all other associations. He made some fairly impersonal conversation about being neighbours, how I should come by for tea sometime (it was obvious he didn't mean this). I said very little, feeling cheated out of an erotic thrill.

The time after that was again in the street. I was on my way to visit my friend who lived in the same building as him. This time the encounter was even briefer than the previous one, more matter of fact, the power of his aftershave erecting a kind of force field between us. When he once more leant in for the compulsory peck on the cheek, the magnetic effect was one of repulsion. I found myself deterred, almost hearing the electrical hum of the current pushing us away from each other. I was angry that he would want to deny me like that. I wanted it to go back to the way it was before. If it ever had been. I didn't know anymore. You can only remember a smell when you smell it again, and his seemed forever lost to the aftershave.

Strangely, by the time I was climbing up the stairs to my friend's flat, the lingering traces of his perfume in the hallway – where he must have just been – actually had the effect of reversing my defensive anger. My interest was re-piqued. My emotional response to the scent had gone through a rapid evolution in the 100 metres between the spot on the street where I had seen him and the hallway inside the building where I was currently standing. The distance between these two places must have been precise, a meticulously calculated stage in a tyrannical re-education of my senses. Torture – brief respite – then a gentler persuasion to the cause. The process had worked in what I imagined must have been record time (I felt weak for not resisting it more), and I was now prepared to put myself in harm's way as if for an unknown but absolute ideological cause. I became convinced the scent was just a wall I had been sent to get on the other side of. Like the clothes of an object of desire one has never seen naked, the aftershave too now seemed to me to be a cloak covering over something indescribably beautiful and intoxicating. And dangerous.

From then on, every cordial touch from him, offered in passing (and as I now realise – in indifference), was incorporated into the mystery, elevated to a sign of an intangible connection that couldn't be known, couldn't be sniffed out. This connection remained unrequited and unacknowledged for some time, and for some time this was adequate for me. Its energies were even and did not intrude on my life. But like all good things, it couldn't last.

Every time I bumped into him, which was frequently, I leaned in greedily, ready to be slapped across the face with the obtuse. Never once did a real conversation ensue. The smell of his aftershave, initially so repulsive to me, was now developing into a tantalizing rejection, a wall against which I felt compelled to bang my head. Was it self-abuse? Or was it something more profound? I began to see political meaning in the impossibility of the exercise. The logic was simple. If the wall cracks before my skull, the order of things in the world will change – patriarchy and capitalism will fall and an unimaginable, better, new world will take their place. And I might finally get to have sex, after all these years.

Then I realised, the aftershave was not an abstract, disembodied force. There was intention behind it. Will. His will. What did he want? Maybe he too had read the article about the dating event where participants could smell the anonymous T-shirts of strangers, and then based on their preference, have the opportunity to talk to their presumed pheromonal match.

Maybe he had taken offence at the clumsy biological determinism of the whole thing. Maybe he wanted to stand up for his socially constructed self, stand up for his ability to choose, be a thinking subject, rather than just be subjected to a reductive idea of biological destiny. And, more to the point, maybe he also wanted to be chosen.

The procedural polite kisses on the cheek eventually developed into hugs. And one evening a crack finally appeared. I am not sure whether the crack was in his defences or in my head, but something definitely gave in. If only for a moment. It was a hot evening, I was premenstrual, and feeling feral in a compromised sort of way. A mix of sexual desperation and hypersensitivity. Ripe. I also felt like the total antithesis of the aftershave. I was initially trying to ignore him. Aside from feeling like a mere expanse of pulsating skin, my sensitive state also made me feel very obvious, and somehow I couldn't help but feel ashamed of the whole thing; for the thoughts that had passed through my head, and the bareness of what I imagined was my current bodily smell, which I thought had no hope of being reciprocated. Then, as the art opening that provided the setting for our encounter was wrapping up, I could no longer avoid eye contact. He came over to the corner where I was hiding behind two acquaintances, squeezed past one of them – with some difficulty – and hugged me. I tried to just do the kiss-on-cheek thing, but he pulled me closer.

And I could smell it. First the aftershave, somehow thinner this time, and then an undeniable layer of heat, of sweat, pushing through. I was not sure that I did recognise it, and it was impossible to know if what I was feeling was raw, undeniable, physical attraction, or the result of a need to be validated that had grown beyond all form, swollen out of the reach of all subtlety. The elaborate thought processes that had, for me, punctuated our encounters, had long since left all hope of reality catching up with them in their dust.

The smell hitherto hidden under the aftershave, initially representing all that was undeniable about the material world, had completed a transformation. The truth of his bodily scent, finally unveiled, was no longer a physical fact. It had become an idea, it had become 'Truth', or even 'Love'. In my lustful haze I misidentified this construct as something entirely under my control, something I had brought into being through willed actions (as opposed to it being a momentary crystallisation of all that had been seeping through my skin, eyes and ears in the course of endless formative experiences and influences). The discovery of this perceived truth gave me a curious sense of omnipotence. ◊

I had to leave to go to a party, and in any case, physio-logical sensations and internal (or merely internalised?) philosophical epiphanies aside, I could see no hope of us speaking to each other beyond the initial greeting. I got very drunk, and my sense of vindication diminished as the night wore on. By the following morning I was truly unhappy, but somehow still holding onto the remnants of potency. Something about this exceptional state of mind was crying out to be exploited. I tried to think it through. I thought, would it really be that bad if I contacted him? I thought, he *did* suggest we have tea, albeit it had been months since the invitation, which, as mentioned before, had not appeared particularly sincere in the first place. Now though, I thought, I could lean on the invitation for strength. So I sent him a brief message asking if he wanted to have a coffee at some point in the week.

I waited for a response. For a day, two days, a bit longer. I remembered a time years before when I had received a rather elaborate email from someone I did not know very well, but who I thought was OK, asking me out on a date. The email had explained how and why he had felt compelled to get in touch with me despite us not knowing each other very well, and how he had approached a mutual friend for my email. At the time I had a boyfriend, not that this was very well known by anyone. The relationship did not end up lasting very long. It did however make the invitation slightly problematic, especially as the email was so direct in tone. It felt cumbersome and presumptuous to respond by saying 'Thanks, but I have a boy-friend', yet it was also the only possible response I could have given, all things considered. So I never replied.

I never received a response from Aftershave either. I was overcome by an urge to apologise profusely, all the while realising this was not necessary, or even sincere, just a sort of watered-down remedy for the pangs of an irredeemable disappointment.

EPILOGUE

Sometime in the future I was sitting in a pub, talking to a few friends. Before I noticed him, I noticed the piercing smell drifting in from somewhere behind me. He had sat down next to one of my friends, and proceeded to address her. Within an instant she had turned all her attention to him, having perhaps (like so many of us) mistaken a penis for the phallus. Reaching out for that thing that no one had but everyone wanted, she began to stroke his arm. I first turned my back to them, and then, unable to shake off the scent that kept wafting into my consciousness, I got up and walked away.

———————

The Aftershave

Note: ◊ In a passage in *A Contribution to the Critique of Hegel's Philosophy of Right*, Marx states that Hegel performs a sort of inversion of subject and predicate – for Hegel the Concept pre-exists and manifests itself through material reality. The Concept is the subject of the sentence, so to speak, while material reality is a secondary term, the predicate. Marx says that this is the wrong way around – in fact material reality pre-exists the Concept – material reality is the 'subject' while the Concept is 'the predicate'. Was this similar to what had happened here? Had the narrator's convoluted thoughts enacted something like this flip? The further into the realm of ideas love travels, away from any actual loving, the more it starts to appear as a universal thing pre-existing humanity and its capacity *to* love. Subjects and predicates become muddled. What was interesting also was that her overthinking the smell, which could have been thought to constitute active reflection, offering some resistance to the biological determinism of ideas of the absoluteness of physical attraction, had in fact managed to mythologise and idealise said physicality to the level of the Hegelian Concept, and as far away from any material basis as was humanly possible.

The Measure of Reality

Emonomics

The woman on the radio was talking with what initially seemed like unusual candour:

> There is a certain economy to relationships, one reflected in the language that often surrounds talking about them. Lets call it emonomics. People talk about 'investing' in relationships, cutting their losses, also the word 'value' (multifaceted as it is) features heavily in all sorts of self-helpish communications. When people consider their sense of self-worth, how (or whether) they are 'valued' in their relationships, nobody ever seems to consider the hard sell, the flogging of your wares in a collapsed market. An object passes the event horizon, into the black hole, without ever appearing to do so to an external observer. I caught myself having a dream in which in an effort to persuade someone to have sex with me, I said to them: 'My father always told me "Nothing is free in this life, but some things are cheaper than others".'
>
> A crisis of overproduction happens when capital accumulated can no longer be invested profitably, nor all commodities sold to consumers. Capital demands profit and the paper value of 'Love' (that most fictitious of all capital) is propped up by destroying the value of labour needed to produce it. Love becomes rarefied when loving comes cheap.
>
> This is the paradox of accumulation. 'Love' needs desire and the means to pursue its objects in order to maintain effective demand, but increasingly has to resort to destroying these in order to valorise itself.

What my father in reality told me was: 'You don't have to do anything in this life except die, and you only have to do that once.'

He didn't elaborate on the temporality of that death, though the sentence does imply he meant something finite, perhaps quick and merciful. He was of course wrong.

An individual might not have to die except once, but the shape and time death takes is less definite. Desire is amortised over long stretches. Further than this, the social sum of slow deaths – you could call it 'aggregate demise' or 'total demise' – overshadows the relative freedom that constitutes the core of this piece of paternal advice.

Marketing yourself for a cheaper price flows imperceptibly into having to 'take one for the company'. An observer crossing a black hole's event horizon can calculate the moment they've crossed it, but will not actually see or feel anything special happen at that moment...'

I heard her go on for a while, then the reception faded out. Or I did. In any case I couldn't follow what it was she said anymore, even if the image of her voice seemed to linger on, getting more redshifted as time passed.

The Challenge

Make a list of all the things you find challenging about your life. The number of challenging things listed is not limited. Challenge your friends to do the same.

I FIND THE FOLLOWING THINGS CHALLENGING:

1. Feeling lonely.
2. Missing my family, and how this cruelly points out the absence of any other context of emotional intimacy in my life, such as boyfriend, children and close friends who don't hate me.
3. Having friends who hate me because I am unable to fill their black hole of loneliness, even though or perhaps because I have one too.
4. That despite getting up around 7am most mornings, I seem to get very little done with my day, and am hugely relieved when it's time to go to bed (9pm).
5. That all my waking hours are spent ostensibly working – but in reiteration of the above, nothing ever gets finished.
6. That the reason I am never not working is that there isn't anybody whose company could make me relaxed enough to constitute real leisure.
7. That most of my work consists of making proposals for things to do in the future, and because my livelihood depends on this propositioning, it takes precedence over any actual realising.

8. That my whole life is a hypothetical proposition.
9. Challengingly bad PMS that gets increasingly bad month by month, indicating entry into the perimenopausal phase of my life.
10. Pretty much the same as above, but fading fertility without it even ever having been proven that I am in any way fertile in the first place.
11. That I haven't had sex in nearly two years.
12. That in the last ten years I have only had sex occasionally, making point 11 not such an anomalous stretch in the broader context of my sex life.
13. That despite the above, I always feel the need to make a concerted effort to render myself as friendly/goofy/ unsexual as possible in social situations so that other women don't perceive me as a threat.
14. That instead of being able to enjoy my still relatively youthful appearance, it leads to a gross paradox of having to experience most of the problems all ageing women face, but without any of the respect seniority (not to mention skills and experience) might and should solicit.
15. That I have a lot of anger.
16. That my friend said my high levels of anger might be down to my Ayurvedic dosha being out of balance and that I shouldn't put so much chilli in my food.
17. This is not so much a challenge in itself, but rather an embarrassment, which I am challenging myself to share with you: yesterday, I watched a make-out scene in Martin Scorsese's *The Departed* about ten times over (where undercover policeman, Leonardo DiCaprio, gets it together with his *therapist*, Vera Farmiga), not because I found it titillating, but because there was something addictive about the extreme sense of grief and loss this depiction of tenderness and intimacy solicited in me.
18. That I know any representation of romance in Hollywood

films is poisonous ideology, yet I was still moved to tears
by the above-described scene (I am challenged by my own
perpetual self-betrayal).

HOW I LIVE UP TO THESE CHALLENGES – AN EXERCISE
IN POSITIVE THINKING:

1. Being alone is not always lonely.
2. Lacking emotional intimacy outside the context of the family I grew up with makes me appreciate their presence more.
3. I can identify with this hatred.
4. I get a lot of sleep.
5. Life is a journey, completion comes with death.
6. Work can give you a sense of (resigned) self-reliance that relationships cannot.
7. I make a living.
8. My whole life is an elaborate and ambitious hypothetical proposition. Ideas.
9. A sense of urgency might spur me to take action.
10. Life still holds at least one enticing mystery.
11. The idea of sex is for me not tarnished by an inadequate reality.
12. Due to their scarcity, I remember all the occasions I have had sex in the past ten years in great detail, and can delve into this bank of memories to find material for tragicomic but ultimately touching stories of fleeting human efforts to connect.
13. I have grown to possess a modest amount of superficial social charisma.
14. People have low expectations of me.
15. Anger makes me feel alive.
16. I now know how to maintain my high levels of anger.
17. After having watched the scene ten times over, and having

The Measure of Reality

cried inconsolably for two hours, I watched it again to take note of the specific pace of its editing. I feel I learned something new.

18. I am able to combine intellectual reflection with immersion in a sublime aesthetic experience.

The Prognosis

Apparently loneliness is twice as deadly as obesity.

She reflected on this curious statistic that depended on the attribution of a variety of ailments to one central factor and a quite subjective one at that. Or at the very least on establishing a speculative causal connection between that factor – loneliness – and causes of death. Exactly twice? How had they come up with a figure, she wondered.

Still, it could not be denied that loneliness had a certain morbidity about it. It made one hyperaware of one's own mortality, and was accompanied not only by sinister thoughts, but also by a range of hard-to-pin-down ailments. The strange connection between loneliness and illness had first come to her at a time right after her breakup from a long-term partner, when she was still sharing a house with him. It had dawned on her that she was alone through an episode to do with illness. In distinction to the findings of the study, however, it had not been loneliness that had made her ill, but merely illness that had alerted her to her loneliness.

She had woken up one night feeling odd, but unsure why. When you are half asleep, things are twisted – everyday anxieties are amplified to the point of representing not problems to be solved but mortality itself, yet one's immediate physical state can be beyond all legibility. You don't really know what is going on with your body. She had walked downstairs to get a glass of water. On the way back up, in the middle of the stairs, holding a glass of water, she had felt faint. She had

The Measure of Reality

dropped the glass, which had not broken. Then, to her complete surprise, she had projectile-vomited on the stairs.

Slowly waking up, she had taken in the quiet house and as she looked down on the moonlit pool of sick, a range of realisations had reached her. The first was that she still felt very ill, the second was that she had a stomach bug, the third that despite the silence surrounding her, her former partner was sleeping in the spare bedroom just metres away from her, the fourth was that it was no longer OK for her to wake him up to tell him she was ill, the fifth was that she was going to have to clean up the vomit herself, and the sixth and most significant of all was that these realisations culminated in the sense of security and closeness provided by the relationship having been irretrievably taken away. She had realised how conclusively alone she was.

From that point on everything became a near-death experience.

The danger of a fall at home, of choking on food, of going to bed too drunk with no one there to place you in a recovery position (or of no one telling you not to cycle home drunk from a party in the first place), of being so excited about getting a text message that you forget everything else around you and walk under a car – being deprived of meaningful human contact was hazardous and she felt in peril. ◊

Some time after the vomit incident, and while still occupying the same-house-separate-bedrooms arrangement with her former partner, she brought someone back to her house that she had met at a party. Someone, a man that is. She did not have sex with him, but as far as the former partner was concerned, or was able to know, she did. She heard the front door slam in the middle of the night. In the morning, he came back, his body entirely covered in all-too-convenient hives. ◊ It might have all been a coincidence, of course, but then again, she sensed that what in psychoanalytic literature is called 'somatic compliance' had always been strongly present in him. ◊ He lay in bed with his mystery rash for three days, and on the third day arose and moved out.

If hysterical symptoms such as these arise partly in order to attract attention, his body had misread her propensity for caregiving. She in fact could not bring herself to care even the tiniest bit. Something about the nocturnal decanting of her stomach contents had withdrawn the ties that bound her to him and that had made her feel responsible for his well-being. Or perhaps his need for recognition had channelled itself into a kind of mimicry. He had identified in her a need to be cared for, which his body had proceeded to mimic. She was a sibling and a parent, with whom he both competed for attention and whose attention he needed. She now recognised the couple form, at least as they had lived it, as a loop where the same finite, often inadequate, amount of attention circulated, kept in motion by a convoluted passing around of roles – roles that were not played, but rather attributed. ◊

This shifting and shirking (ultimately of blame) was given a comic edge by the way the roles thrown about like insults never seemed to coincide with their purported players' self-perception. Just as she thought of herself as a responsible sister, she was accused of being a (bad) mum, and so on. But somehow these sketchy identities had still seemed better than none at all. The fact that what they consisted of came from someone else, someone committed to this task of labelling, made them more real and valid than if they had been a product of self-invention. Self-reliance was a pipe dream, external validation (whatever shape it took) – or the absence thereof – was all there was.

Loss of a specific close relationship initially led many people to amplified efforts to get the missing attention back, from all possible quarters. She had noticed it was people who had recently become single that seemed to most need nursing

The Measure of Reality

from their friends while ill. The shock of there really not being anyone to automatically take care of you anymore, not necessarily, not without asking, not without several text messages sent to several people, in the hope they might respond or offer to bring some food around, made their need deeper than it had ever been previously. What eventually followed was resignation and the advent of dull and hard self-sufficiency. But before this happened, right before, people sometimes had minor accidents. Not entirely on purpose, not entirely as a cry for help or in an effort to attract attention, but more in harmonious physiological compliance with their dark thoughts. Spilling boiling water on yourself, cutting your hand in the course of food preparation, twisting your ankle while stumbling on the stairs, none of these came with the expectation of attention. In fact they might go unreported for several days. There was something uncontrived about the reception of empathy-interest accrued during the days between injury occurring and friends finding out about it and offering their horrified sympathies. Ultimately, many even acquired a kind of pride in their loneliness, its rationalisation as something hard-won. People were sad about their loneliness and sense of isolation, but held onto it as if it were the last possession of any value they had left. They never called, they rarely picked up the phone, and if they did make efforts to see other people, they were very selective about who they saw, and spoke only about the people they were unable to see (and how not seeing them made them feel lonely).

Keeping fit was also a paradoxical aspect of the pathology of loneliness. The heightened awareness of one's body brought on by the newfound sense of vulnerability, required it be cared for and bolstered against any and all possible harm. 'Taking care of yourself' is something that becomes less an advisable thing to do, and more a necessity, when there is no one around to care for you. This involved an escalating paradox. The more you invested (time and money) in your well-being, exercising, eating expensive organic food, taking dietary supplements, making getting enough (in reality probably too much) sleep your daily priority to which everything else, be it work, friends or family, deferred – the more you felt like you were falling apart. And the more your 'taking care of yourself' became an agent of your isolation.

Her condition bore some fleeting similarity to that of the American boy who could never go to the doctors. Physical, moral, and mental hygiene appeared to both her and the American only achievable through an extreme form of disconnection, yet it was the absence of love, of any kind, given or received, that was the most dangerous thing of all. The saddest thing about her adoption of this disconnection was that without knowing it, she had placed herself apart from the ascendant norm and on the losing side. Those with more astute survival instincts aligned themselves with select intimates, at any cost, and quite rightly so. The only thing that could save anyone at this point (or postpone the moment of their demise) was a retreat into the closed circle of a family; the social contract masquerading as biological destiny.

She found herself declining invitations with increasing frequency when they did come in, thinking her peace of mind the final priority. She wanted to protect herself from the mental agitations and paranoia that came with having to enter into social situations as a free agent, without being sure that anyone had your back, that anyone was guaranteed to be a benign presence. Without these assurances, everyone was presumed to be a malignant force instead. It was safer to presume this. It was safer to stay at home.

Not being able to muster the energy to apply her precious 'peace of mind' to creative tasks constantly, she carved herself leisure time within her home, her relaxation consisting of streaming television series online. The series offered stimulation in a manageable form, in a form that did not make any demands

The Measure of Reality

of her, that in fact did not pay any attention to her whatsoever. These days, when she got ill with a cold, she no longer felt sorry for herself that no one was around to feed her painkillers or to make her cups of tea. In fact illness in a way provided a temporary release from the guilt of never leaving the house, and a license to totally immerse herself in whatever programs she was following at the moment. The cocoon that had coiled around her – its surface thickening slowly and unnoticeably until it was hard and impenetrable – left her exposed. There remained little to be done, so when each new wave of illness – real or imagined – washed over her, she did nothing to resist it, but instead closed her eyes and obligingly pressed against it, as if it were the caressing hand of a lover.

Notes: ◊ Being driven to despair by loneliness was like a spiral where one bad panicked decision followed another, and led one to the most surprising, overblown, dark places. One example was a story she had once heard, of a friend of a friend, who after years of resisting the urge had signed up for Guardian Soulmates and who within an hour of joining had received fifty replies from men she would never have even remotely considered in real life. Most of them seemed well over fifty, even though she had specified her age range as '25-45'. She had not understood that being just over thirty-five herself, she had passed the magical line of eligibility, the sell-by-date, to use a worn expression, of women in the online dating game (and that some people lied about their age on their profiles). Not being in the best of states to put this assault on her self-image into perspective, her self-esteem eroded by years of 'dignified' solitude as well as tragically tied to external assessments of her attractiveness, she committed suicide.

The Prognosis

◊ Her partner had expected all women to care for him like his mother, and confronted attempts at doing so like a child in a certain stage of development would a mother – with an effort to destroy her so as to assure himself that the mother was resilient against these efforts. He wanted to destroy the mother and know that the mother would not be destroyed. This was exhausting. For all concerned. Not being a child anymore, there seemed to be no hope of a transition into a more sustained understanding of the mutuality of this negotiation – there was only repetition, a conflict raised over and over and over again. A need so profound it could not possibly be met.

◊ Somatic compliance in the context of hysteria means an actual pre-existing condition that becomes psychically amplified into a fully blown symptom. Freud writes about greedy little girls: 'The motives for being ill often begin to be active even in childhood. A little girl in her greed for love does not enjoy having to share the affection of her parents with her brothers and sisters; and she notices that the whole of their affection is lavished on her once more whenever she arouses their anxiety by falling ill. She has now discovered a means of enticing out her parents' love, and will make use of that means as soon as she has the necessary psychical material at her disposal for producing an illness.' Sigmund Freud, 'A Fragment of Analysis in a Case of Hysteria', Volume 5 of the *Standard Edition Complete Psychological Works Of Sigmund Freud* (Vintage Classics, 2001), p. 44.

She had MUCH empathy for 'greedy little girls', yet when it came to her (former) partner who obviously fell within the parameters of Freud's use of this category, she had none. This absent empathy was a source of some momentary twinges of bad conscience, but also gave rise to a rather cruel sense of triumph.

◊ In unpacking Freud's famous *Dora* case study (from which the above quote originates), Juliet Mitchell discusses how Dora's symptoms seemed to be imitating the physical illnesses of her female family members, and notes that these illnesses all seemed to be related to their relation to men – gonorrhea, syphilis, an aunt's mysterious wasting disease attributed to an unhappy marriage, a cousin suffering gastric pains out of jealousy for her sister who was about to get married. She writes: 'We could say then, that the currency of sexuality in Dora's family was not that of a sexual or reproductive body, but that of the sick body'. She later adds: 'Freud posits sexual fantasies as lying at the root of hysteria and that hysterics mimic other people's desires. I suggest that the late nineteenth-century hysteric specifically mimicked not just sexuality, but, overwhelmingly, the sexuality of the endlessly sick body.' *Mad Men and Medusas*, pp. 87-88.

She thought that today the economy of sexuality was based on a paradox of lack and abundance different but strangely analogous to the nineteenth-century one described by Mitchell, in as much as sexuality (as so many aspects of life) could be said to symptomatically manifest the structural sickness of the economy. The currency of sexuality in contemporary western (capitalist) societies was also not of a reproductive body, but of a sick one: the economic system did not reproduce itself, but consumed itself from the inside. The desire for desire that had defined twentieth-century consumer culture, extending to the way sexuality had been commodified and how its commodification had conditioned private sexual behaviours and predilections, seemed to take a further leap into hysteric territory in a recession. The early twenty-first-century hysteric both suffered from and mimicked the individualistic scarcity they saw all around them – economic and romantic.

Own Worst Enemy
(The Rat Woman)

In the dream her hand was hanging over the edge of the bed and a rat came along and bit it. She screamed and shook her arm to try to make it let go, but this did not help. Things got worse. Her entire hand was now consumed by the rat – the inside of its stomach felt scratchy. She woke up to find her hand lodged in her own armpit. She was pressing her arm down tightly to prevent her hand from escaping. After a brief struggle she manage to wrench the hand free from her own grip, but it had gone to sleep and she had no control over it as it flew through the air. It hit her in the face. Very hard.

Severance

Dear so-and-so,

I am writing to you in regard to my
recurring bouts of cystitis. I am
concerned I find myself wanting to
inflict harm with alarming frequency.
It seems it may be the only way to
impress upon you just how painful this
is. I suspect you have been told by
scores of past girlfriends to watch not
to transport faecal bacteria anywhere
near their urethras. Girlfriends who
undeservingly would have felt self-
conscious that they were 'killing the
mood' or being pedantic or overly
clinical in warning against this – only
to be ignored because you had no idea
not only how painful but also how
tedious having small insistent urinary
tract infections is, how much it puts
you off sex, what a hole it corrodes
in one's ability to get things done
and feel good about doing them. In this

respect, I have come to imagine you as a sort of latter-day Typhoid Mary, a symptomless carrier of disease (though of course you are not a 'carrier' in a medical sense, your actions merely facilitate its onset). Also the way you seem fixated on the very solipsistic male fantasy of the multiple female orgasm unnecessarily prolongs the inter-course, causing friction that adds a further element of risk. Just because something is possible does not make it universally preferable.

It all makes me think of an episode of the 1980s TV series *The Ray Bradbury Theater*, in which a man looking into accidental road deaths discovers that the deaths he is investigating could be traced to the interventions of a mysterious gang of people, who would arrive at the scene of a crash and in the guise of helping the victims, move them around, poke and prod their bodies with the intention of speeding up their demise before the ambulance crews arrived. That is what our sexual encounters feel like to me right now – furtive agitation, physical harm dressed up as good deed: the superficial appearance of benevolence underpinned by malicious intent. It could be that I am overreacting, but this is what the

niggling insistent pain does to you, the
having to get up at 7am to queue outside
the health centre in the cold, with the
spewing and coughing and limping crowds,
in order to see the doctor for what is
deemed a minor complaint.

I also find myself increasingly unable
to enjoy sex – in any conventional sense
in any case – because my attention is
drawn to your hands and what they are
doing. More specifically to the
direction of their movement. A constant
vigilance about where your hands have
been and where they are and where they
are going forms an entirely independent
sphere of action in my head, separate
from anything I have learned to think
of as sexually arousing. It's all about
territories, about what kind of bacteria
is friendly where, and where it is the
enemy. Dirt is only matter in the wrong
place. Perhaps this is a sign of the
limited nature of my thinking (because
really, why fear bacteria? Why not let
it gently take over, give ourselves over
to its/our destiny. Isn't life just a
futile battle against being overcome by
it? A kind of violent resistance to a
natural order – though I have to say,
I don't think such a thing exists). Now
reflecting on it, there is something
about this transference of concen-

The Measure of Reality

tration, away from the erotic nature of the situation into an all-encompassing anxiety about bacteria, that constitutes an erotics of its own. A novel form of sensuality based on a heightened state of alertness, on the thrill of managing to keep your wits about you in a dangerous situation. Still, this is a bigger thrill than what I had bargained for; more than I can currently fit into my life. I hope you understand why I feel compelled to sever our arrangement. It is not personal, so please don't question yourself. Not that you were going to anyway. I am sure you will have no trouble finding new employment elsewhere.

Yours,

PS: Should you require any references, I am happy to lie on your behalf.

Notes Toward a Case Study
(or, The Analyst)

The conflict present in a child being toilet trained, originating
in the contradiction between being told not to pee or shit
in the bed, while being told to pee and shit in the potty –
pee/don't pee – persists in his sexual behaviour.

It is not that he is fixated in the anal stage of psychosexual
development in the Freudian sense – he is neither anally
retentive nor anally expulsive, but he isn't able to occupy the
ground between them with any comfort either. The persistence
of this stuck ambivalence between retention and expulsion
can be most clearly detected in his dealings with women. For
someone with such an expansive ego, he has unusual trouble
with balanced regulation, and his sexuality is marked by
indecision between excessively loose and excessively controlling behaviours. He is overly seductive, striving to turn every
innocuous situation into a sexually charged one, swinging in
every direction, causing mess and disruption, yet this is paired
with a strange unwillingness to let (himself) go. ◊ He is a
distant sexual partner, and it is difficult to make him ejaculate.
It is as if he were holding onto his semen as punishment, or
possibly in a desperate effort to retain some moral dignity.
Another line of inquiry into this could be that this semen
retention is to do with a form of disguised sadism. In prolong-
ing the intercourse he can be mean (in both senses of the
word) under the guise of wanting to please – the discomfort

experienced by his partner as a result of the porn-standard fuck-length might in fact be, at least unconsciously, something he is seeking to inflict. Somehow the phrase 'boring someone to death' comes to mind.

It should also be noted that the secondary site of manifestation for this dual position is speech. He will talk about things pertaining to what he terms 'stuff' (cultural objects, theory, basically anything not pertaining to subjective experience) ad nauseam, yet when it comes to expressing any of his feelings with the help of words, he becomes verbally retentive. It may be that this has to do with a social prohibition against showing weakness, but it seems it is also consistent with a strong urge to control his environment, something for which he nevertheless possesses inadequate regulatory tools.

One wonders if this isn't also a sign of the times.

The ability to control one's bowels and bladder is an integral stage in the child's development. Previously this could have been taken to entail an element of socialisation – by learning to control your actions you were also conforming to society's norms. Now a (well-documented) shift has occurred. Perhaps what is so striking about his behaviour is not that it contradicts the social norm, but rather that it conforms to it, in that the social norm has itself become antisocial. Forms of self-control previously viewed as healthy are not encouraged. Being a responsible adult resolved into coexistence with others is suddenly no longer possible, or even desirable. We are constantly drawn to extremes, and the contradiction between the two poles is the only place to exist. Sex presents itself as abundant, but yields nothing. It is everywhere visible yet also everywhere absent. There is a nominal freedom for everything yet the means for nothing. And what is most damning, the imagination for nothing. Without imagination there can't be desire.

The imperative to be sexually liberated forms the dominant ideology we live under, which he for one seems to have at least superficially lapped up. This tyranny of enjoyment, as most of his peers know, is one of the hardest things to live up to – all but impossible. The real source of his problems lies in his obstinate blindness in the face of this impossibility – his lack of imagination for different ways of being that kills desire. He thinks he needs to attempt to fuck every woman he meets, but aside from the quirk of his moral/libidinal conditioning preventing him from ejaculating (in an involuntary, neurotic sort of way), the blatant improbability of being able to enjoy sex with an entirely indiscriminate selection of people manages to escape his attention.

There is a childlike disappointment that follows finding pleasure absent where he thought he left it, paired with a senile insistence on repeating the act over and over again (he is stuck in something misleadingly resembling the fort-da game, repetition and play as a way of controlling painful experiences, but he lacks the child's self-awareness and ability to learn – instead, his repetition is a simple having-forgotten, or maybe a not-wanting-to-know).

Even as a symptom, he becomes a culprit.

———

Note: ◊ Really some might say that his behaviour was, well, hysteric (and what of the analysts?). Juliet Mitchell remarks that the acknowledgment of the existence of the male hysteric led to the normalisation of hysteria, its reimaging as a post-modern individual. She writes: 'Today's hysteric is an everyday Don Juan (male or female) – creative but seducing, lying, someone for whom death has no meaning, transmitting jealousy and chaos wherever

The Measure of Reality

they go.' *Mad Men and Medusas*, p. 38. Hysteria is no longer a clinical condition; it is a cultural condition.

The hysteric as having been dispossessed of their ego further illuminates this point. The 'times' the sign of which the analyst was discussing, was an era of inflated yet insubstantial egos. Like the images of 3D cinema, where the illusion of volume was continually intercepted by moments of disorientation and the appearance of flat planes, showing up the 3D images as bodies without matter, surfaces without substance, so too the egomania that was everywhere made no secret of the absence of an ego at its centre. At best the ego was weak and hungry, constantly looking for others to feed off, to adopt as extensions of itself. At its worst, or perhaps most radical, it was entirely absent, and people became nothing more than the symptoms of the overarching trauma of the culture they lived in.

Finding The Words

I was flicking through a book, trying to find the sentences I knew I had seen there, and which I knew would prove my point. The task was time-sensitive, and I grew increasingly flustered with my failure to locate them, scanning my eye across the pages faster and faster. This obviously made dis-covery ever more unlikely, the exercise ever more futile. The sentences were ringing through my head, but I could not catch their meaning – they had to be matched to visual proof in order to make sense.

The Annals

> *In fact, the annalist's account calls up a world in which need is everywhere present, in which scarcity is the rule of existence, and in which all of the possible agencies of satisfaction are lacking or absent or exist under the imminent threat of death.* ◊

The number of tabs open on her browser was dizzying. A man she had once been in a relationship with, briefly, had found this irritating and disorderly. His fondness for order and lack of complication irritated her in turn. The relationship was short-lived and though the breakup had been superficially amicable, there was a sense that underneath it all they both found each other fundamentally alien and disagreeable.

There were many reasons why some tabs were never closed. These included the difficulty of letting go, the illusion that one might still at some point return to these past moments – whether in time or inquiry – the keeping alive of questions that had passed through one's head, but that due to lack of time or concentration were never delved into with any dedication (which they purely by virtue of having been asked now seemed to deserve).

Or maybe the significance of the open tabs was as Hayden White writes of medieval annals: 'Their importance consists of nothing else but their having been recorded.' ◊

709. *Hard winter. Duke Gottfried died.*
710. *Hard year and deficient in crops.*
711.

712. *Flood everywhere.*

713.

714. *Pippin, Mayor of the Palace, died.*

715.

716.

717.

718. *Charles devastated the Saxon with great destruction.* ◊

TAB 1: *Home –BBC News*

TAB 2: *Latest News, Sport and Comment from The Guardian*

TAB 3: *Facebook*

The tabs certainly did form a curious kind of record of history, a story waiting to be told, links and connections and causalities waiting to be drawn. Links, connections and causalities that would never be drawn.

TAB 13: *Explore the British Library*

TAB 14: *My Reading Room Requests*

What could be said of the central subject of the tabs, of their collector? For one that their initial curiosity was greater than their ability to sustain an interest. Their melancholy bond with their past whims was evidenced in the tabs, which conveyed a hunger for specific information, but that was, as a whole, essentially without specificity. Unscrutinised and rarely revisited, they constituted a life lived as a summary glance.

TAB 6: *Interview with Elfriede Jelinek (on Ingeborg Bachmann) Part 1*

TAB 7: *We Are All Clitoridian Women: Notes on Carla Lonzi's legacy*

TAB 9: *LIES final download single page*

The Annals

Whereas the annalists' recording of years signalled 'the fullness and completion of the time of the Lord', the open tabs gave off the appearance of time standing still, time that the tab collector wished to possess and freeze, time that would never be up, events never subject to retrospective wisdom, forever current. Falling somewhat short of this ambition, the tabs nevertheless continued their existence as a bizarre sort of objectivity, a map of the narrow subjective path taken by their now anonymous accumulator. They hovered on the screen, occasionally having to be restored after the computer crashed. The freezing of the screen, and the subsequent recovery of the tabs, was metonymic of the collector's broader aspirations: the entry into a suspended state where going back remained an option (though one never taken up).

The confused regret deriving from never having made a choice about the direction one's life should take (spurred on by a lack of acceptance of the fact that with some things no amount of choosing was going to secure a planned outcome) was seemingly redeemed by the open portals.

The tabs represented the potential not only for the possession of ever greater wholes of knowledge and greater depths of precision and detail within those wholes, but also the possibility of holding onto every option that had in reality already been lost. The actual effect of the tabs was the opposite of their promise. Their potential was inextricably tied to the impossibility of its actualisation.

TAB 26: *European Sperm Bank – Fees*
TAB 21: *Permission Slips*

The tabs were like a testimonial to a form of dementia. They were opened, and once they were hung in their place on the screen, they could be forgotten. They *were* forgotten.

TAB 27: *Kathryn Bigelow – Nicholas Ray: The Last Interview*

The possibility of the simultaneous hovering of open tabs made remembering unnecessary, and eventually impossible. All that was needed to comfort the prematurely senile mind buckling under the weight of what *could* be had was the occasional note taken of the continued openness of any one tab. This state of flotation complemented her romantic disposition, or more to the point the way it had some time previously started peeling off the surface of reality, the objects of her affection becoming simultaneously more distant and more close. Located inside her head, they could not have been more attuned to her emotional intricacies. Her love life was now situated purely in fantasy, and there was a certain harmony to this. Her fantasies of love hovered between the world and her ego, and between the ego and its destruction.

TAB 29: *Is It Love?* ◊

This delicate balance could not last. Her gradual resignation was sped up by the rapid decline of her brain, as she turned further and further inwards. There was something of this giving up on the world crystallised in the empty constellation of information. The question remained, did the still barely present attachment to these markers of investment in the outside world constitute introversion in Freud's sense, the withdrawal of libidinal investment in objects in the world in favour of those existing solely in fantasy, or did it go beyond this? Was it narcissism proper, i.e., was all interest now directed at the collector's ego? ◊

TAB 28: *I Am Someone, Look At Me*

Or was it worse than this? Was it the erosion of the ability to desire at all?

Conversations with other people became difficult, as nothing was processed or retained by the individual mind. ◊ The hypothetical accessibility of information, and by extension meaning, caused permanent damage to the brain. Forgetting why you had wanted to read this or that article, watch this or that video clip, graduated into an inability to recognise the relation of words to each other, of images to their broader context. Forgetfulness became a kind of aphasia. Names began to disappear.

Eventually all words became unrecognisable.

TAB 30: ...
TAB 31: ...

The Measure of Reality

The Annals

TAB 33: ...
TAB 33: ...
TAB 33: ...
TAB 33: ...

The blinding horror of everyday existence that might have been at the root of the medieval annalists' lack of narrative agency – for whom 'social events are apparently as incomprehensible as natural events' ◊ – could now be observed in the passivity of the tabbist skimming over a reality they had no part in. Things happened, they were held by the annalist of the tabs, but she was not their agent. The central subject of the tabs does not 'do', their only verb is 'browse'.

TAB 33: *Portal*
TAB 34: *New Tab*

Notes:
◊ Hayden White, 'The Value of Narrativity in the Representation of Reality', *On Narrative*, W. J. T. Mitchell (ed.) (The University of Chicago Press, 1981), pp. 1-23, p.11.

◊ Ibid. p. 8.

◊ From *Annals of Saint Gall*, quoted in White, 'The Value of Narrativity', p. 7.

◊ Sándor Ferenczi wrote to Sigmund Freud: 'You speak of two kinds of "end of the world" (that of dementia and that of being in love). The world actually gets lost into dementia, while being in love has to do with the end of

The Measure of Reality

the ego, which can nevertheless bring with it no lesser cataclysms and can be just as revolutionary psychically as the regression to narcissism is in dementia.'
Eva Brabant, Ernst Falzeder, Patrizia Giampieri-Deutsch (eds.), *The Correspondence of Sigmund Freud and Sándor Ferenczi, Volume 1: 1908–1914* (The Belknap Press of Harvard University Press, 1992), p. 557.

◊ In 'On Narcissism', Freud writes about dementia praecox (a now outdated clinical term for a mental disorder entailing loss of cognitive abilities and effecting young people – 'premature dementia'. It later became interchangeable with schizophrenia). Freud finds both dementia praecox and schizophrenia lacking as definitions, and combines them (though only in this text) under the term 'paraphrenia' (not to be confused with the later use of this term, which refers to psychotic conditions that include paranoid delusions but no loss of cognitive ability). He makes a connection between dementia praecox/schizophrenia and narcissism, and writes at length on the withdrawal of libidinal cathexes from the world and the replacing of object-love with ego-love that occurs within these conditions.

◊ She had considered sharing the content of the tabs on Facebook or on Twitter, thus ending their determining power over her life. A restoring of her life in the outside world of sorts. She could read them, or she could just post them without reading them. The effect would be pretty much the same. It would be a simultaneous (exhibitionist) claiming and expulsion of the thought contained by them. If she read them, she could even understand them in passing, but there was no need to really think through this understanding, no need to remember it, once it was placed in her digital mirror. Being released from the pain of thinking was the immediate reward, while being seen to have read the articles was a validation of her proprietorship over them. She could have them but she wouldn't have to think about them or through them. But somehow this all seemed too easy. Aside from a certain vanity that prevented her from revealing so much of her tastes to the world, there was still something in her, some fledgling desire for 'true' engagement with thought that she was not ready to be liberated from. So the tabs stayed for a while longer, awaiting the final crash.

◊ White, 'The Value of Narrativity', p. 7.

It's Not Too Late!

It's not too late to find love. It's not too late to start preparing your life for a better future. It's not too late to choose to have a different (better) life. It's not too late to choose. It's not too late to make the conditions inside your head more hospitable to others. It may be too late to make the conditions inside your womb hospitable to a fetus.

It's not too late to try to hold onto the things that have already passed. It's not too late to deny their passing. It's not too late to think it was your fault. It's not too late to regret not doing something you never even knew you wanted. It's not too late for regret in general. It's not too late to make the locus of your disappointed, objectless hopes something that you could never have had in the first place – or if you could have, would have left you with other things to regret. But for some things, it really is too late.

In the pages of the inflight magazine of a budget airline, she found the two adverts, a spread away from each other.

Hair and babies. For the youthful but ageing, mobile but financially struggling generation of Europeans these may just present the epitome of aspiration. In this respect the placement of the adverts made sense, but from the point of view of actually selling anything, it did not:

It's not too late to have a baby!
(Advertises the Swiss fertility clinic.)

The Measure of Reality

It's not too late to stop hair loss!

(The promise here seems even more intangible, the claim harder to verify.)

Babies and hair. One is new life, the other is dead matter pushing out from your head (it could be cut without bleeding, they said it 'grew', but it was not like animals or plants. It was in some ways an unlikely symbol of vitality. It was an indicator of life or the stage a life was at, but it had no life itself – there is a reason why shampoo adverts say 'healthy-*looking* hair').

'Are you making something new or merely trying to hold onto what you already have?'

Single, childless men passing forty have crushes on girls in their twenties (who they may or may not be able to attract). Women think of the possibility of a late-life baby, which (if only they were not on this flight, betraying their lack of means) they might be able to afford. Instead they end up dating men in their twenties, who are too young to want to father children, and too full of something to fall in love.

Both men and women worry about losing their hair.

Even if you do not earn a lot of money, you may be persuaded to part with a large chunk of it, if it is to service the hope that doing so might keep the remaining hair on your head from falling out. You can't afford to be any less attractive (not anymore).

As for fertility treatments, thinking of children as an investment in your future is so third world, yet isn't that exactly what this constellation of elements was conspiring to assert? On a purely aspirational level, of course. The equation:

Budget airline (= Lack of funds meets the need to be constantly on the move, presumably for work purposes; being on the go has also made it difficult to form lasting, supportive relationships) + It's not too late (= You are of the age where you worry about your future; your reproductive capabilities are fading, in both senses of the word) = Appealing to people's undefined need for security, loving and being loved dovetailing into an idea of being established, entrenched in affection and care (given and received), tethered to 'something good' by bonds of mutual dependency.

Any dependents? No, but it's not too late. ◊

She recalled correspondence she once had with a friend about the similarities between the plot lines of two films released in 2013, *All is Lost* (Robert Redford lost at sea) and *Gravity* (Sandra Bullock lost in space). A segment in one of her emails to him read:

> *'When you describe Robert Redford's mask-like expressions, it makes me recall thinking there was something blank about his face, as if he was suffering from dementia and every once in a while would look around in this empty panic, having forgotten what was going on. Like ageing as an apparent, superficial refinement of your "personality" (the deep deep character-filled, caricature-like wrinkles) that belies its total cancelling out. In fact, ageing as a cancelling out of any dignity (or gravity) that one might have expected from it in accord-ance with popular mythologies, or even past truths.*
>
> *When you think of this in relation to* Gravity, *there is something interesting about the similarity of the main characters – one a woman in her forties and the other a man in his seventies. Not in the sense that these are equatable based on the gender difference – as in a 45-year-old woman is the social equivalent of a 75-year-old man (though sure there are people who would argue this is the case). I think it's more interesting to think that this reveals there is something ageless about the ageing process, a cultural condition that erases the kind of definition between the different stages of life that*

The Measure of Reality

would have existed previously. Like that in (for want of better words) post-Fordism, late-capitalism, post-crisis capitalism, there is something that makes a person who would previously have been a productive adult in their forties, more like an elderly person infantilised by their dementia.

The whole absence of reproduction – there is only survival masked as mystical rebirth – is interesting too. Sandra Bullock is mourning the loss of a child, but in some ways it's almost like whether or not there actually was a child previously is sort of irrelevant. What is really being mourned is the absence of the possibility of having one (she is definitely past the age this is possible anymore). All that is left then is to give birth to yourself. And in the process she becomes a grown-up baby (like you say, gasping for – its first? – breath). Sandra Bullock would be space debris herself, the empty shell of floating matter, if it weren't for her innately human capacity of self-reinvention. But a reinvention that leaves her bare and facing evolution all over again. And you're right, there really should not have been any dialogue, at least not after the initial pre-space-junk-disaster scene.'

It now occurred to her that both Sandra Bullock and Robert Redford have a lot of hair. George Clooney has a lot of hair too.

Her own parents' investment in her did not seem like it was going to bear fruit. She was unlikely to ever be in a position more financially secure than them. They themselves of course were more of the thinking that their sacrifices meant their children could freely express themselves, be unbound by the economics of familial reciprocity. Any investment in the future had been in themselves, for the benefit of their children, rather than the other way around. Whether this attribution of value to self-expression as the ultimate point of upward mobility was a feature of their generation, or just a personal

It's Not Too Late!

fancy, the conditions making it increasingly difficult to practice such a disposition were of an epoch-defining magnitude. Not only did the changes in these conditions mean that taking care of your elderly parents was back on the table financially, but they had an effect on the delicate structures of emotional reciprocity, too. ◊

There were too many frustrated self-realisers around, poorly socialised and unable to stand each other – whose creative ambitions and powers of self-realisation were tested daily against economic realities. The odds were not in their favour. She was not the only person she knew in their thirties who spent periods of time living with their parents. Many of her peers did the same, often for a few months during the summer, when work pressures were a little less intense, and when being in attendance in a big city (whichever one it was) did not seem so integral to their 'careers'. Mostly it was a matter of saving money on rent. For her, though there was a rationale of convenience (she could surely not hold down a flat in every country she had business being in), further justified by the temporary nature of such stays, there was more to it. There was a closeness, that after years of difficult and disappointing intimacies felt like coming home – even beyond the literal meaning of the words. The family ties that had at some point felt constricting, needy, unchosen, now seemed to present something stable in a world full of fleeting attachments and fickle affections. They represented the only remaining site for real closeness. This was something that she had had an inkling of for years, an uncomfortable truth subtending all appearances, but the difference now was that it no longer looked like a failure, something that would need to be kept out of one's consciousness. On the contrary, the surfacing of this suppressed knowledge was a relief, an eventual clarity in a muddled situation where no eventualities had ever even been considered. ◊

The Measure of Reality

There was a melancholy empathy that accompanied these sojourns. It was as if at the same time as she regressed into a teen-like, dependent state, she also became fully mature, finally seeing the similarities between herself and her parents. She was able to co-habit not only their house, but also their vulnerability, the weaknesses that made them human. Her parents had both recently retired, and there was something about the idle confusion that came with the change in their circumstances that echoed her own existential state. Seeing them potter around the house, not really sure what to do with their days, going for the occasional walk and spending a lot of time thinking about food (and spending a lot of time on the computer), was not that different from her own house-bound yet oddly boundless existence. The space shared offered a protective shell, where they all fumbled along, not talking to each other much, but aware of one another's presence. A presence that reassured them that they had not yet fallen through the cracks.

She had thought of how old people were often encouraged to 'keep themselves active', or how you sometimes heard them attribute their relative youthfulness to the same, and found it both tragic and hilarious that this seemed to be something that she could think of as a guiding principle of her own life too. She was also concerned with 'keeping herself active', with occupying her body and mind against the sedentary odds, so as not to lose all her will to live. In many ways she had often felt like a solitary pensioner, rationing the social engagements available so as not to use her weekly quota up in any one go. Even during periods when her social life could be said to be very active, she still spent the majority of her time by herself, thinking ahead to trips to the shop and anticipating the swim she had scheduled into her otherwise structureless day. She had made this connection in a slightly jokey way, but never before had it become as tangible as it was now that her rhythms became synchronized and co-ordinated with these actual retirees, the parents.

And there she was, sitting on the plane again, waiting for the seatbelt sign to be turned off so she could get her computer out. In the meantime, not having brought a book to read, she was browsing through the complementary magazine. The strangeness of the two adverts provided a stimulating distraction from the otherwise boring content, and the observations and chains of associations that followed from them made her feel like she was fast accruing invaluable new perspectives on the world. And her own life in it. And on how it was unlikely that she would bring any life beyond her own into it. This was not so much a resignation as it was an acknowledgement of a certain winding down that was taking place.

Then, for a moment, she couldn't remember where the plane was heading. 'Where am I going again?' she thought, and had to concentrate all her mental energy to recall, aided by the clues provided in the magazine, the answer to the question.

Notes: ◊ There was something sinister about advertising the idea of a family to someone travelling on Easyjet, but why was this really? What were the implications? Promoting family, or the possibility of one, in general seemed to have a relation to a broad cultural sense of loss. Loss of reason, or of the family as a symbol of reason, an agent of socialisation. Commercial idealisation of family seemed to play on a nostalgia for an imaginary past rationality.

The Measure of Reality

Aimed at someone who always took the cheapest possible flight (regardless of the discomfort this might entail), it might have meant something else. It might have signified the one thing they were unable to have, providing a focus for a more nebulous and general sense of loss. The only thing available for them to actually consume (seeing as actually having a family really did seem impossible) was the ideology emitted by the advert. Just the *idea* of family, thanks, none of the substance. They were able to breathe in a promise of the regulation absent in their own lives. The precarious itinerants' hunger for control (and for being controlled in some tangible way, in a way they could see and touch and be able to process and perhaps rebel against) was fed with the fodder of a lost order. The family as a symbolic structure through which partial autonomy from authority is gained (according to Freud) represented the possibility of simultaneous belonging and independence, and what remained of this idea in the fertility advert soothed the drifters' pervading sense of being cast adrift.

◊ Was there an increased significance to family, and what did it mean? In the Nordic countries people were having more babies than before, but what was this really? A frivolity? A kind of 'because we can' (so comfortably)? Or was it slowly turning into a last hurrah in advance of the death of the welfare state that people were intuiting might be just around the corner? Soon they would REALLY have to start having babies, as all the while it would become (be made) more and more difficult to do so. Everywhere else, the process was already well underway, and the rise of the significance of having a family was more acute, more serious. It spanned across the collective consciousness: from the dawning acknowledgement that the majority of wealth, which it was already known was in the hands of the very few, was now growing exponentially into a small number of inherited mega-fortunes, to its more humble manifestation, the increased need for the less fortunate to rely on their families – parents, children, siblings – for mere everyday survival.

It's Not Too Late!

◊ Well, her giving into the realisation that her family was the only place left to turn for closeness, wasn't exactly just a relief. There remained a sort of ideological guilt, a nagging feeling that there was something wrong about this feeling of belonging. Or if not wrong, then at least false (though wrong too, as what else were families than the manifestation of some boundary, a device for policing the terms of inclusion and exclusion: us and them). Was she kidding herself? She recalled that Georg Lukács wrote about a state of transcendental homelessness defining modernity, a state of constant longing for a place one once belonged to, particularly observable in romantic literature as a wish to return to nature, spurred on by a sense of alienation from the man-made world ('second nature'). Adorno negated the possibility of a return, as for him this homesickness for an authentic origin was also a part of second nature, and a product of modernity. 'Home' had arisen out of its own absence, 'return' from its own impossibility. The nostalgia for family as a place of belonging, 'a home', she thought, conformed to this structure, to this gravitation toward a lost origin that had never really been there to begin with.

The Measure of Reality

I'm OK, You're Not

At some point the scales had tipped. The way people used to talk about what they did, driven by a need to convince others of their excellence, had now turned into an effort to convince themselves. There was a timbre to their voices that made them sound like they had lost the plot somewhat, and every sentence that came out of their mouths sounded like it could have been replaced with just one, to be repeated over and over again: 'I'm OK. I'm OK. I'm OK. I'm OK. It's OK. I'm OK.'

The Psychopaths

The reason she was not in a relationship was simply that there didn't seem to be the minutest instance of ambiguity, the smallest opening that would allow her into one without going through such profound humiliations and compromises that, when 'settled', there would be anything left of her. She had known only a handful of men who didn't come with a blunt sense of emotional entitlement, an all-out stupidity when it came to themselves that allowed them to think that they were the captivating heroes of their own lives, for whom all those around them existed. It wasn't really even narcissism – they didn't see other people as continuations of their subjectivity, but they did fundamentally see all women as somehow having a duty of care toward them (with some personal variations and quirks to make the whole thing less simplistic, more convincing and human). She had never been in or witnessed a heterosexual relationship that wasn't a pit of murderous dependencies – sometimes well disguised but still present – that stripped men of their self-knowledge and deprived women of the last remnants of love and affection: the recognition they might have been able to just about squeeze a drop out of more fleeting encounters. She had never had or witnessed a heterosexual relationship she wanted to be in.

Other women compromised, in stoic solitude put in the emotional efforts that should have come from two people. Put in the work required for them to claim their reward. This was the sacrifice they had to make, the price they had to pay for their sexual desires that had the misfortune of being long since fixed on the opposite sex. She tried to stay open, to suspend her disbelief in an unbroken trust and sense of solidarity between men and women. Whenever she made this effort, to firstly be unsure rather than fully negative about a situation, and then give something, anything, to it, her generosity was met with total presumption on the part of her *potential* lover. Every kind word she offered, every effort to inject a sense of sexual excitement into an as-yet-to-be-decided connection, was taken as a sign of her undying love or erotic obsession with her counterpart. Worst of all, it was taken as a promise. Everyone is always misunderstood, that is the way human communication invariably operates. But to be misunderstood to such an extent – to be misunderstood and, by this, be dismissed in one arid sweep of vacuity, was simply unacceptable. To be misunderstood and have the carefully cultivated environment where something might happen, where some feeling or sensuality could take place, be so crudely trampled on. She just did not want to continue wasting her life in this way. Men seemed to have nothing but contempt for women, but very few of them ever realised this (and the ones who did were proud of it), instead thinking they were sensitive, that they came equipped with the full complexity of human emotion.

It's not that he was particularly interesting, that his emotional life was so rich and surprising that it demanded description. Quite the contrary, actually. He was almost too easy to read. Missing much of what might have been considered a standard understanding of nuance when it came to the ins and outs of sexual relationships, he was articulate to the point of meaninglessness – something that did not only extend to his assessments of others, but was also somehow constitutive of his own emotional landscape. He was a blunt object, inflicting blunt-force trauma void of all ill intentions.

He seemed to not simply embody, more just be, the exact median of some otherwise unverifiable masculine personality flaw – the one everybody knew *was*, but were ashamed to admit knowing about or to attempt to describe, lest they be accused of being reductive or gender-essentialist.

He gave license to describe. He *was* the generalisation, the rule, all the disappointing things you expected from men but still managed to be disappointed by, regardless of having gone looking for them. He was nothing and everything: every cliché, every innocently self-regarding romantic narrative, every man pursuing their own bombastic, and in the end by necessity tragic, love story. Every effort on the part of his lovers to insert their viewpoint, themselves, the incongruity of their desires into his obstinate equation, to communicate the existence of a disjointedness that was indeed in the heart of any relationship – and that one should not be afraid of – was met with a wilful and keen translation of this difference into some identity of understanding (his), a fated-by-god harmony of minds and genitals. Every time she attempted to open a space for something real to happen between them, a space for some sort of encounter, he just poured into it, filling it with his projections. Far from being from Mars, he was something between Jupiter and a black hole. A gas giant that would devour you without anyone on the outside ever realising that you were gone, or if they did, being happy for (or envious of) you because they presumed that it (he) was objectively desirable.

There was something in his libidinal makeup that allowed him the illusion that he was a friend to women, that his tastes were not informed by dominant representations of beauty, that he could offer something to the underappreciated, somehow excusing him. To everyone but him this was however just another, perhaps even more crass than usual, form of objectification. He enjoyed 'characterful' features in women – the more chiselled the better. If it wasn't written in huge red capital letters in a visible place, he simply did not see it, let alone understand it. She was put off by his poor powers of observation, yet found them calming. His preference for boyish girls had also always seemed quite misogynist to her, even when she had been the doubtful beneficiary of this predilection, years previously. At a time when she had been so unhappy that she had become emaciated, losing most of her feminine physical attributes, weighing in well below a healthy BMI and having cut her hair very short in some depressingly formulaic effort at renewal, he had found her irresistible. To her this had been partially comforting, while at the same time being transparently self-serving and ignorant of her needs – perhaps of her subjectivity altogether.

These days, beyond the constant empty assertion of an empty agreement, he seemed so ill-prepared to extend any enthusiasm toward their situation, preferring instead to hedge, that there was no way she could find herself in any way excited about him either. In keeping his options open, he was in fact closing them all down, one by one, not having understood that attraction is never entirely one-sided, and that for all their ability to love, most people's affections had some core element of narcissism, that on some level they were sparked by the way a relationship or another person allowed them to see themselves in a new, favourable, light.

She met up with their mutual friend. The friend kept mentioning his name, repeatedly inquiring into his well-being. It became apparent to her that some transmission of information had taken place. Her imagination of the shape this transmission would have taken was painful. She pictured him coquettishly weighing up the outlook for the union, as if he had any intentions of persisting with it (he did not), more concerned with appearing somehow 'normal' or honourable in his friends' eyes than with being honest about what was actually going on.

This assigned the fragile threads of a dawning understanding between them – the understanding that their affection for each other had inbuilt limitations – a secondary role.

Such understandings were, of course, dependent on both parties viewing the other as having entered the situation eyes open, so to speak. She remembered a time, once, when in the middle of the night he had turned over and grabbed hold of her. He had put his arms around her, and though it was awkward – her arm was in the way, she couldn't comfortably respond to the gesture – squeezed her firmly and with some desperate urgency. He kissed her head a few times to express the bottomless depth of his need for closeness. This call for intimacy was completely out of place in the context of their relationship. She realised he was (half?) asleep, and she was suddenly overcome by feelings of tenderness. She thought she could recognise this state of having drifted into an entirely different realm of consciousness, perhaps having a dream of being in love, of experiencing sensations that could not be carried over to an awake state – they were so limitless and without form, that when one woke up, they receded with enormous speed (like a vampire scuttling from the path of light), chased away by the laws of cognition and physiology. The tangibility of these feelings was painfully poignant in its impossibility, with the brief moment of stirring from a dream providing proof of both what could and could not be had. He no longer seemed as callous as she had judged him to be, as marked by shallow affect, or as led by vanity. He was merely alone, much in the same way as every one else was.

He had then regained some degree of consciousness, loosened his hold, and gradually, with meticulous intent, turned away from her.

A few days later, they had a conversation about the way people seemed often to be entirely transparent about their deepest aspirations, however nominally contradictory these

The Measure of Reality

may be with their willed, surface-level actions. And about how comical this was. She paused for a while, and then brought up the somni-cuddle, feeling around for a playful tone. Both to prevent herself from becoming one of the involuntary emotional exhibitionists they were talking about, and in order not to hurt him with the implication that he was (though this was the implication). His response too aimed at finding cover from being cast in this role. His scrambling effort at owning his actions went something like, 'No, I think I remember that. I was awake.'

They both knew this was a lie, and there was a sad sense of embarrassment that accompanied this knowledge. For him, the sadness/embarrassment came with the realisation that he did not indeed have any romantic feelings for her, or any feelings of an intensity demanding tight embraces filled with longing. For her, it was to do with his failure to recognise her empathy for and identification with the need-without-an-object his unconscious embrace had expressed, and how for her, this identification had constituted a bond of sorts between them. A bond that his lie – or rather his lack of sophistication in identifying the more obvious answer as the correct one – seemed to undermine. She felt embarrassed for him.

Talking to the friend, she now thought she understood something further about this brief flicker and subsequent extinguishing of connection between them, its place within a larger set of dynamics. Events that did not have her at their centre. She saw that the understanding between them was inferior to the love between men shared by him and the friend, however based on an exchange of convenient narratives and flattering self-representations this love may have been. Not that she entirely believed in the friend's culpability in this charade. He seemed sincerely delighted at the idea that she might have been seeing *him*. Something about the optimism of this friend's prying, calling out muffled from a distant place she had no access to, cauterized the trickle of feelings that had unnoticeably begun to flow from her into her dealings with *him*. The friend was a good person and life responded to his goodness with happy outcomes. The impossibility of her even imagining this place he existed in, where love wasn't terrible and mired in inflated, omnivorous egos, but was kind and mutual, and more to the point where things transpired, revealed itself as the ultimate block, the boundary beyond which her confused sensations could not spread. She responded to his implicit question even more indirectly, with something that was not about her but still clarified that his joyous expectation of a new pairing was unfounded. The friend politely let the matter be. Politely or out of a lack of any insistent interest in how things actually were? Part of what made him so wholesome was his ability to let things lie, to not get caught up in things that did not yield to him with a gentler sort of push.

She had never learned to expound before she met him (not the friend, *him*). A proto-neoliberal critic of neoliberalism, he had first introduced her to the practice of being a winner. The necessity to assert oneself against his endless drivel of me-talk, the listing of his accomplishments and schematic summaries of the world (for which he used big, schematic words), had since made her a master of the not so fine art of listing her achievements and projects to even the most fleeting of conversation partners. Talking to the friend, it occurred to her she couldn't change herself back. She listened to the deadening bullshit of her own spoken curriculum vitae, ◊ unable to stop its flow or find any point of connection that wasn't promptly flooded and drowned out by the sound of her own voice.

Maybe she had become one of them, the psychopaths, the entire generation of middle class people living without meaningful bonds and being somehow largely oblivious to there being anything wrong with this. Nominally creative and

The Measure of Reality

constantly on the go, they were the cosmopolitans for the austerity era, who had become deranged by the constant insecurity and weight of competition under which they lived. They stubbornly held onto the perception of themselves as middle class, whatever the actual poverty of their circumstance.

The friend did not seem to possess this feature of constant self-proclamation characteristic of the psychopaths, and this was what made him so loved. Though perhaps ultimately this love he enjoyed was in many cases merely a kind of instrumentalisation. His non-competitive streak was interpersonal gold, a rare commodity that everyone wanted to benefit from. People identified their love for him through the absence of hate, an emotion that was established as the base level of feeling as far as their peers were concerned, the burn of petty gripes and envies making itself known at the first moment they opened their eyes in the morning (the black and whiteness, the polarity, the un-nuanced clumsiness of the love/hate dichotomy was also indicative of the poor quality of reflection that defined their times). They identified love in their absence of hate for him, but this was not the cause of their love. They loved him because he allowed them not to hate themselves so much. He both exposed and redeemed the egomaniacs' underlying insecurity in one benevolent nod of his head.

And insecurity was everywhere. One of the effects of a highly competitive environment was the lack of peer-to-peer affirmation. No one complemented each other, unless it was to get something. As a result, no one ever felt important to anyone else, and this formed a feedback loop between people's unhealthy self-interest (self-interest itself is a good thing, within reason, it had just become entirely distorted) and a decline of any real form of self-esteem, something dependent on affirmation. The competitive environment forcibly inflated everyone's egos, while brutally hollowing them out. ◊

She also loved the friend, but felt ashamed of this because she feared it meant that she too belonged to the new phallic breed, that her love might ultimately be shown to consist of nothing but vanity and hot air. So instead of the friend, she opted for *him*, not him to keep or to love, but him as a reassuring means of measuring her own contempt for herself. That and as a potential sperm donor (however, she had not committed to this plan). ◊ She resisted the urge to offer the friend her version of events, to yield to his gentle probing and clarify the matter. In so doing, she also thought of herself as extending some sexual solidarity to *him*. It seemed like the right thing to do. Or at the very least the alternative (the use of her sexual liaison as a tool for bonding with the friend) seemed wrong. Even if *he* didn't understand that whenever you have sex with someone you accepted some small responsibility for protecting them from exposure, she did.

As a few days passed, the words inside her began to swell. She began to care less and less about what the dignified (or right) thing to do was, and more about just being able to talk to the friend without her second-guessing getting in the way. And about claiming her corner. The opportunity to undermine *him*, to put herself ahead of him had presented itself and she had not taken it. She felt she hadn't really said what she had wanted, and the need to speak and to express herself, to be listened and responded to (something he never did), was becoming unbearable.

In the end she buckled and wrote the friend an email, disingenuously apologising for having been abrupt. She hadn't been, she had been perfectly smooth, ever the seasoned psychopath: *'but, it was because...'*. She said how annoyed she was that *he* had divulged anything, and how her imagination of how he might have presented the situation had gotten the better of her. The friend replied promptly and with genuine-seeming concern. He was sorry she was upset, but that if it

The Measure of Reality

made her feel any better, nothing had ever been discussed between him and *him*. Apparently they did not generally discuss such things.

Though the revelation that what she was unflinchingly sure had happened in fact had not, should have been a little humiliating, it wasn't. Seeing the ridiculousness of her self-assured convictions had somehow the opposite effect. The effect of lifting her out of the sea of perceived slights and unfavourable power dynamics that she had trained herself to watch out for, sometimes to the point of bringing them into being. As with a dream of love that recedes at the point of waking up, she now felt like something was escaping her understanding, that the thing that had been so close and important to her was being stripped away. But instead of leaving her maimed beyond repair, there was a relief. She was released from the shackles of her own significance. She really did not matter, and this was OK. Better than. In an environment where everyone fought so desperately to be somebody, to be special, this sense of being nobody felt satisfyingly counter-cyclical. And in any case, her time would come.

———————

Notes: ◊ What misleadingly beautiful two words these were: *Curriculum vitae*. They sounded so liquid yet resonant, as if one's life were a mountain stream, vibrant and determined, directed yet unafraid of exploration, dynamic but buoyant and lighthearted, never ever having to make too much effort. How incongruous these sounds were with the actual meaning of the words.

◊ It occurred to her that this space void of acknowledgement was similar to the one in which women had been forced to live throughout the ages. Institutionally deprived of affection and affirmation, as one half of all people they had proved their superiority to the aggregate of the whole in not having become as marked by ruthlessness. Still, she could identify the effects of this sad deficit in relationships between women too. Women too on occasion hated other women, perhaps for not possessing the social power to affirm them.

◊ One of her problems was the absence of sexual union that might produce children. She kept telling herself it was ultimately all within her power to control, if only she approached it in a sufficiently pragmatic and systematic way. But... really, at what cost? The amount of purposeful wilful decisions one would need to make in order to even get to that situation. Pursuit of pregnancy for someone who rarely had sex presented a feat of organisation, a mound of logistics and careful planning. Money spent and no guarantees. Now that she had half-accidentally started having sex with *him*, her thoughts turned to trying to utilise the situation somehow – but ultimately it was just a thought experiment with no real life application.

The Measure of Reality

Dialectics

A pregnant woman is standing on the street. She reaches into her bag and pulls out a tub of pills. She pours some on her hand, and puts them in her mouth. She senses that she is being looked at by the miasmic civil police whose watchful eye reserves special attention for pregnant women. She is visibly irritated by them. She turns to me and says, defensively: 'I'm on dialectics!' Somehow this is understood to mean a type of medication that will help dilate her cervix so as to bring on labour. It didn't really make sense, the pun, but she was so adamant that I just accepted it.

The Profiler

If it is the fixed order of property dependent on settled life that grounds the human alienation in which originates all homesickness and all longing for the lost primal state of man, it is nevertheless the settled life and fixed property (only in which the notion of a homeland can appear) to which all longing and all homesickness are directed. ◊

It seemed to happen with increasing frequency that she found herself on the page. She had forgotten how she had ended up looking at this particular Facebook profile. Probably there had been a comment on a mutual friend's wall that had caught her eye. A comment that was a little bit clever, but not too brilliant, amusing but not ecstatically observant. Then, without her noticing, the profile had somehow become a point of stability in her life. At the end of each day she found herself needing a peek into its alternate reality. The life represented on the profile, the house, the kids, the adoring friends, the nice-seeming wife, were all too conventional to actually elicit any desire, too ordered to want to live. What it did stir was a painless lifestyle envy – it was pleasurable and comforting to pore over it, but it also did not exactly make her feel the anxiety of having made all the wrong choices or make her feel that the rather intangible things represented by the profile had forever slipped out of her reach. On the contrary, the profile gave her a curious sort of access to these unspeakables. All the things that she was unsure she wanted (or that she had

The Measure of Reality

decided against, but still felt an occasional pang of regret about having missed out on) were there. They were presented in a compact, distant, yet oddly intimate form. Tuning into the profile had a calming, almost euphoric effect, where the problems of her own solitary life faded into the background, but without the real commitment and responsibility that having a family and holding down a job or a marriage would have required. It was 'just' a fantasy, but one with real life application. She knew that family life (or love) was not going to cure her loneliness, but a fantasy of it might. At least it operated in a remedial capacity just fine.

It wasn't that different to watching your favourite TV series, or consuming any other form of immersive fiction, but for the distinction that the Facebook friends she shared with this person made the aspirational narrative appear more reasonably like a part of her reality. It seemed somehow more relevant to her needs and interests too. The possibility of possessing the lifestyle depicted was more apparently present and the people seemed more accessible. The life sketched out in the profile wasn't outlandishly glamorous. She recognised many aspects and details of it from her own experience. All these minutiae served to create a veneer of participation – participation in the life of someone she had never met and of whom she ultimately knew nothing of any import about.

Every time she saw a 'like' on his wall from someone she knew, her mind drifted away into reveries of a different life, one that was both in the past but perhaps also in the future. He lived in an area in which she too had lived, and frequented a pub that had been situated downstairs from her flat twenty years ago. The updates on his house renovations reminded her about her own efforts at the same, years previously, and though she had long since condemned such nesting activities as a waste of time and creative energy (the ultimate unpredict-ability of relationships having provided many an example of the true precarity of any domestic dream) she still felt a longing for all this nonsense, as if for an imaginary past, a false memory of a more innocent time. It should also be said that he lived in the country of her birth, which she had long since abandoned. ◊ And where she might yet return. The sense of looking forward came from a suggestion of a life yet to be experienced that the example set by the profile provided. A life still achievable if whims of chance chose to throw her that way. He was a proto-type, someone who she might become, or like someone she might meet and settle down with. Rather than seeming exceptional in his own context, he gave the impression of being prevalent and widely available, therefore providing temporary release from the all-permeating sense of but-I-never-meet-anyone.

Though it had not escaped her attention that all the ful-filment provided by her checking-in activities was entirely dependent on a blurred distance, of details that were lacking details – context lacking context – she *did* however seem to be able to forget that there was a flip side to all her pleasurable hypotheticals, and the conditions that enabled them. The flip side being that she knew nothing about this person really, and that the proximity that made him seem somehow familiar meant that there was a real chance that she might indeed one day meet him. This was an eventuality that she had not accounted for.

During one of her visits to her hometown, she had arranged to meet a new acquaintance at a cafe. She still made an effort to meet new people, to convince herself that she was interested in the world and to feed the illusion of progress and change in her life – change, that is, beyond the slow but reliable decay of her body. The cafe they met at was in a neighbourhood where she used to live. She knew it from before but hadn't been in there for years. It was unchanged, and had a simultaneously bizarre and endearing '90s-throwback feel about it. It was aspiring to be 'European' in a way that had long since become redundant, the distances between countries having become smaller through increased mobility. Or, if it was presumptuous to talk about the increase in actual mobility, not everyone having the means or the lifestyle allowing for much travel, then at least it could be said that virtual mobility had changed the way people perceived themselves and their relation to the wider world around them. The last time she had been in this cafe, she had just been connected to the internet in her flat for the first time. She and her friends had gathered around the chunky taupe computer monitor with its curved glass front, and attempted to figure out what this new thing everyone was talking about was really for. They tried to think of things to search for, worlds to discover, but everything they thought of yielded poor or no results. They were puzzled by all the hype around what essentially seemed like an incredibly dysfunctional phonebook. Now, the world outside having moved on from the 1994 of the EU referendum and landlines, the Parisian vibe of the cafe had become unveiled as the figment of someone's very singular and vivid imagination.

As she sits talking with her new friend, a man and a woman walk in. She notices them in the corner of her eye, but does not recognise them immediately. As they approach, having been waved over by her companion, she realises the man is the hero of her favourite profile, and the woman is his wife. Her initial shock comes when he opens his mouth, his voice higher and more nasal than she had imagined. This is very disappointing. The two men (her new friend and the man from the profile) start a friendly but semi-professional-sounding conversation. At first she tries to follow what is being said, to contribute a clever remark or two, but these remarks get stuck in her throat. Her conversational fluidity is soiled by the putrid shame swilling around in her gut. The knowledge of her secret affair with this person's Facebook profile is too much for her words to overcome.

In fact, beyond initial introductions neither of the women say much. Both the man and the woman seem a bit boring, not like anyone she would be interested in befriending. This is perhaps somewhat harsh, but she has found that questioning her first impressions of people in the past has simply led her on long and fruitless detours into the wrong alien territory, detours which she has always regretted and which have simply obscured her sense of what she was supposed to be doing, or even what she was supposed to find pleasurable. She observes the woman's body language, and the way she follows her husband's gestures and words with an absentminded look of approval on her face. Despite finding this irritating, she recognises something in her reticence, something like an uncomfortably familiar comfort in withdrawal. It seems as if she is hanging back on purpose, using her husband as a shield against a world she is tired of dealing with. The locus of her imaginary intimacy now moves from him to his wife. She now not only feels close to the wife, but feels she knows something significant about her. Her eyes move down to where the man and the woman appear to be holding hands. As she looks more closely, she notices that their hands are not touching. They are suspended in a strange frozen pose, palms facing each other, fingers slightly bent, as if they were two spaceships whose attempted docking had failed. Transported away from the clamour of the cafe and into an infinite, airless space, their extremities were now resigned to hovering in proximity of each other, awaiting further instructions.

———

The Measure of Reality

Notes: ◊ Theodor W. Adorno and Max Horkheimer, *Dialectic of Enlightenment* (Verso, 1997), p. 78.

◊ Homesickness or nostalgia can only be experienced from a distance to its object (in its literal sense nostalgia means homesickness: *nostos* = 'return home', *algos* = 'pain'). In homesickness, the home is forgotten and replaced with an imaginary object. The object is constituted as a relation of intimacy and the absence of the alienation one feels from one's immediate surroundings or situation. By virtue of being far away, the home comes to be perceived 'closer to one's heart' than it ever was.

Her feelings were slightly more complicated than this... For sure, the fact that all this imagery of 'settled life' that she secretly pleased herself with was at a safe distance was the very premise of her vague longing for it, as well as being the premise for this imagery acting as a kind of soft nostalgic lens through which she observed her own past. However, this yearning and sense of intimacy never quite crossed any pain thresholds. There was only a kind of limbo where nothing was felt very strongly, nothing was mourned, desired or loved – merely consumed.

The Traveller

She is in her old bedroom. Her mother can be heard moving around in the adjacent room, going through drawers. She is with her friend, who is angry and tearful, accusing her of sleeping with her husband. She is profusely apologetic and feels tremendously guilty. She is also uncomfortable about her mother possibly overhearing the scene. She feels guilty but doesn't remember sleeping with the friend's husband, which makes her feel worse, out of control. She never actually doubts her culpability. The friend shows her one of the husband's notebooks – it's a bit like a diary of an indie teen poet, involved, in an adolescent sort of way. The friend points out a section in which he has detailed his crush on her. It talks about her hair. She feel a momentary thumping of deep happiness, she wants to see more but can't, her mother is calling out for her and there is so much distraction. The friend says she can't be guiltless (unnecessarily, she has not denied her guilt at any point). She must have done something to solicit his affections, though there is nothing in the book that would indicate this as anything other than his private thoughts. She goes to see what her mother wants. The mother is holding a folder, a catalogue of her parents' VHS collection. Mother opens the folder, points at an entry and tells her she has filed *Mighty Aphrodite* in the wrong place.

She goes back to her room. The friend is holding up a shoe as if it were a question. She responds: 'Yes. I have been all over the place.'

Amorosis Fugax

A strong egoism is a protection against falling ill, but in the last resort we must begin to love in order not to fall ill, and we are bound to fall ill if, in consequence of frustration, we are unable to love. ◊

'Do you want a glass of water?'

He gets out of the bed with some efficiency, as if to signal an end to proceedings, a shift into a different, less familiar, mode. She is feeling lazy, but thinks she probably should go along with this, follow his lead. She is feeling indifferent to him, and does not want her laziness to be misinterpreted as some wish to prolong the moment of coital togetherness.

'Yes, sure.'

He returns and she takes the glass from his hand. She has a sip and then puts the glass down on the bedside table. He is sitting on the bed, again, communicating with his body language that it's time to go. He looks at the glass of water on the table, and moves it.

'It was going to get knocked over.' She raises her eyebrows. 'You put it right on the edge of the table.' 'Oh, did I?' she responds, absentmindedly. 'I should get on,' he says. 'Ugh,' she thinks.

She gets up, gets dressed and leaves. She stops to buy a coffee on her way home. As she is walking away from the counter she notices a young man approaching. He seems to

The Measure of Reality

be on a collision course with her. She thinks to herself how it's funny, how men never seem to make way. They are so confident that the other person will execute the necessary manoeuvre that it doesn't even occur to them. Their right of way comes ex officio, so to speak, by virtue of their institutionalised maleness. Conversely, however hard she might try to bump into this man, to concentrate her mind on sticking to her trajectory, she would still instinctively turn sideways at the last moment, maybe rise onto her toes, and make herself scarce – to no acknowledgement.

These thoughts went through her head, and while they did they seemed so self-evident and foregone, that never did it even occur to her to actually assert some wilful resistance to this phenomena, to put her own presumptions to the test. Had it occurred to her, she would have thought it spiteful and banal. In any case she was in a hurry and holding a hot drink. There was no sense in risking delay and spillage. She approached the point of hypothetical collision with the full intention of stepping out of the way. As the moment arrived, her body did instinctively what it had always done, and she dodged

Something was amiss. Instead of her usual rehearsed gracefulness, the tired but always precise dive to the side, she somehow clipped the man's shoulder with some force. Her coffee spilt and burned her hand. Her initial reaction wasn't one of pain or anger or even irritation, but of surprise. She had not seen it coming. She had been completely confident that she had cleared him.

'I'm sorry!' — 'No it's OK, I'm sorry!' It was like a poorly written scene from a romantic comedy. Something about the formulaic nature of the situation demanded it be followed through, however, and the two struck up a conversation. This compulsion overrode her urgency to get wherever it was she was going. He bought her another coffee, and they retreated to a park bench nearby. She found him attractive, though it

Amorosis Fugax

was obvious they had nothing in common. He had calm deep-set eyes, and a slightly obnoxious beard, and she wondered what kind of a jawline it was hiding.

He says, 'I hope you don't find this rude, but I like the way your eyes point in slightly different directions. I can't tell if you're looking at me, it's quite tantalising.'

She wasn't looking at him anymore. She also wasn't really listening.

'I'm sorry,' she interrupts, 'I know this is a little weird, but do you want to have sex?'

She could have reached for his hand, or leaned in for a kiss, or performed any one of several more subtle actions to move the situation along, but progress was not her primary motivation. Something about the encounter compelled her to stab it in its cute little face. Had she used the word 'fuck', it might have sounded too sexy, try-hard, as if she was trying to perform the role of a sexually liberated woman, sounding out feisty words in a thinly veiled effort to excite and please the man, pander to his lazy underdeveloped plump fantasies. 'Have sex' was about right. He wouldn't say no to it, but he wouldn't be fully drawn in either. He would feel something had been overlooked, but he wouldn't be sure what it was, and he wouldn't be sure whether to blame himself or her for this. He would do it, but it would leave him with a chill, a hollow space in his centre that would slowly start filling up with the cement of too much reality.

After they have had sex, in her apartment, as they are lying on her bed, he asks her if she wants a glass of water. 'This isn't your house,' she thinks to herself, but to him she simply says: 'Yes, thanks.'

He goes into the kitchen and returns with a glass of water, handing it to her after having taken a sip of it himself. She drinks from it and reaches over to put it down on the bedside table. It misses the table and crashes onto the floor. He jumps

The Measure of Reality

up, eager to be of help: 'Stay there! I'll clean it up' and 'Watch out for the glass!'

She again thinks to herself 'This isn't your house', as he rushes to find some cleaning equipment. She gets up, steps over the broken glass and goes into the bathroom. She looks at the mirror, examining the deep vertical lines between the eyebrows, where the involuntary grimace on her face was digging in for a permanent stay. She looks in the mirror and sees that appears slightly cross-eyed. This is new. She covers her left eye with her hand, and notices that her field of vision is not reduced. She covers her right eye and everything goes black.

Holding back her tears she asks the man to leave, and makes an appointment with a doctor.

At the bus stop she is flustered. She wants to be alone and she wants to talk to someone. Probably not a real someone, but an imaginary one. Someone who wouldn't challenge her every word but wouldn't be too keen either. Someone intelligent and responsive, someone who wouldn't take themselves too seriously but who wouldn't hate themselves either. Someone who would have the patience to let her finish a sentence, however tangled, vague and long it was, and however many times she had to restart it from the beginning when she discovered halfway through that it wasn't going where she wanted it to. Someone who would NEVER try and finish her sentences for her.

Somehow the dialogue in her head just isn't flowing. Conjuring the right kind of exchange with the right kind of fantasy-object to ease her mind is simply beyond her at this very moment. She wants to know when the bus is coming, and she approaches the only other person standing at the stop, a man.

'Did I just miss the 30?'

'It hasn't passed in the ten minutes I've been here,' he responds, nervously, but with an effort to sound jovial and cheery. His voice is a little breathless and stammery. She thinks 'Get. A. Grip.'

Amorosis Fugax

She then realises that his vaguely pleased discomfort is not caused by him being somehow automatically titillated by being spoken to by a woman, but is informed by where she is standing. She is awkwardly close to him. Nothing dramatic, just a little too close. This is not intentional.

Through her newly blind eye and the change in her depth perception attached to it, she seems to have relinquished control of her body. This is in some ways distressing, but there is also something liberating about it. The ingrained self-policing of one's physical being has been jammed, intercepted. The power of intimidation she was discovering in her encounter with the random man at the bus stop felt good too. She was now less panicked about her eye.

Then her sight returned.

'We need to wait for some tests to come back, but based on my initial examination and your other symptoms, I wouldn't worry too much. This kind of monocular temporary loss of sight can be caused by a variety of factors. I am finding it difficult to attribute it to any embolic, ocular or neurological origin, so it could be it has something to do with strain. There are some studies into that. Have you been straining in any way?'

The doctor was a young, affable woman. The fact that the doctor seemed younger than her made our protagonist a little sad. Not untrusting, just filled with an acute sense of the worn frivolity of her own life. It was also obvious from her choice of words that the doctor did not share her feeling that indeed every waking minute was strenuous.

'No, not really.'

'I know it sounds ridiculous, but it could be related to having sex... Such cases have been reported at any rate. But like I said, let's just wait for the results to come in.'

On the street again, she thought more about the sensation she had felt at the bus stop. The strange conflicted feeling of

The Measure of Reality

heightened physical presence in the world, of occupying space, of making her presence felt, while at the same time being more out of touch with it and its expectations. Being more within herself, withdrawn into herself, like an aggressively expanding no-go zone. It felt right and she wanted to feel it again.

For some strange reason she had not noticed when the blindness had first set in. It might have been during sex. She liked to close her eyes, to block out the presence of her sexual partner, so it could be that the change occurred at one of those times, making the transition slightly less obvious. This shutting of one's eyes now seemed like a pale imitation of the glorious detachment achieved through the loss of sight in just one eye.

She was willing to take a risk on the doctor's hypothesis.

People always told her that if you are a woman, you can always get laid if you want to. 'If you want to...' Revulsion at the presumptions held within this statement had always prevented her from engaging with it. It was basically saying that if your life, as a woman, was lacking in physical intimacy it was because you were on some level 'too picky'. As if having sex with someone, anyone, who would have sex with you, however repugnant they might be to you, would be an equal experience to having sex with someone you wanted to have sex with. As if it were a matter of simply not wanting 'it', whatever 'it' was, enough. Now however, the thwarted logic at play there was revealing, for the first time ever, its usefulness. It did not seem so important right now who it was she had sex with. Any enjoyment in the sex or intimacy was not the goal here.

The goal was to bring about amaurosis fugax. (She had looked up the medical term for her condition. *Amaurosis* reminded her of the French word 'amoureuse', being in love, or the feminine form of 'lover'; 'woman in love', perhaps. In fact *amaurosis* derived from the Greek for 'darkening' or 'dimming'. *Fugax* was Latin for 'fleeting'. So there was something to be grateful for, in love and blindness.) She wanted to see if she could master this loss of control over her body. Regain her body by losing the conditioning it had been subjected to her entire life – if only for a matter of a few minutes or hours. So she set out to 'have sex'. This time it was not a whim, it was a method.

***

Afterwards, in a hurry to experience the world of public spaces anew, equipped with her new vision, she turned down the offer of a glass of water and rushed out. She walked around, enjoying a new kind of peace. She felt undisturbed by an awareness of her surroundings. She felt confident staring at people without fearing they would call her up on it. They might feel uncomfortable but would not really be able to tell whether she was or wasn't looking their way. Occasionally she bumped into things, or handed money to a shop assistant in an awkward way, almost missing their hand.

She is standing in a supermarket queue; the man in front of her is fidgeting. He puts his hand on his hip, and twists the bent arm backwards, leaning out slightly. His elbow is touching her chest, and she realises that he is fighting for space. She had, yet again unintentionally, been standing too close, and he was now trying to make this known without engaging her directly. She finds this amusing and decides not to budge, preferring instead to wait and see what he will do. The queue moves forward and he moves along with it, leaving a still larger gap between himself and the person in front of him than the one there had been previously. He is trying to lead by example. She moves forward too, ignoring his wordless instruction, all the while unable to help but smile to herself. He turns around. 'Do you mind?' To which she feigns ignorance: 'What?' — 'You're standing a little close... Sorry but it's making me feel a little

The Measure of Reality

crowded... Really anxious actually.' The last sentence is in excess of what she is expecting to hear, and sounds genuinely pleading, vulnerable, underneath the jovial delivery. 'I'm sorry, I didn't mean to. I don't always judge distances correctly. I recently lost the vision in my right eye and everything is still a bit off, spatially speaking.' This is a sort of half-truth. Encouraged by what appears to be a mutual exchange of TMI, he says: 'Well maybe the correct distance isn't always the right one.'

The two walk out of the supermarket together. On the street they continue to chat. It is an easy and honest exchange. Again, the specifics of what is being said remain elusive.

She wasn't sure what she thought of him. And this was OK. She was relaxed and though she didn't feel any powerful physical pull toward him, she was perfectly at ease with waiting and seeing if something transpired. He felt comfortable to her, and talking to him was effortless and could have gone on forever. There was something about the way he looked that did not inspire any immediate affection or lust, he looked like a stranger, but regardless of this she did not feel compelled to shut him up or down, to push him away. Things were fine as they were. She had her eye focused on him.

Then, she started to feel her field of vision beginning to broaden again, as if a blind were slowly opening.

As they were walking and as her peripheral vision returned, the outside world began to make itself known. Light became too bright, even sounds became louder. She couldn't concentrate on what he was saying anymore. The most disturbing thing, however, was her revenant awareness of how she appeared to others. Whether she was actually looked at or not, she suddenly became preoccupied with this thought, concentrating on the sidelines of her field of vision, straining for her consciousness to reach the shadows that stirred

Amorosis Fugax

there. The balance of power was slipping out of her favour. She needed to weigh herself down to stop all this from happening.

She grabs hold of the man's arm to stop him. She pulls him closer and kisses him. He seems surprised, disappointed even. Not just because his noble role in this delicate building of trust has been denied, but also because it feels to him that a beautiful situation has been subjected to an underserved punishment. And that he couldn't but go along with it. He decides to forgive her for this, and make the most of what is about to happen, to fend for a mutuality that was threatening to slip out of (his or their?) reach. Surely it is within his powers to regain if only he is sensitive and present enough.

After they have sex he holds onto her. She likes it, but she likes the black screen sweeping over her eye even more. She asks him for a glass of water. He returns with one, and she has a sip. She then places the glass on the bedside table. He lies back down next to her. He then reaches over her body to push the glass away from the edge of the table.

After a while she picks up her phone, which has also been resting on the table, and instinctively brushes her hand against her nose before swiping the screen with the same hand, all this happening in one continuous movement. Her finger leaves a thin trail of clear, relatively inoffensive but still out-of-place snot on the screen. She retches a little as she wipes it off, contact with the device having transformed the substance from something she had just a second ago touched willingly, if instinctively, into something revolting. As she takes note of how dirty and marked by fingerprints and tiny flecks of some unnamed muck the screen is, some intangibly brief thoughts about contagion rush through her brain, leaving it as swiftly as they had entered. She looks at the screen, which is now illuminated. There is a missed call and a voice message. Still in bed, she listens to it. It is from her doctor. She is asking

The Measure of Reality

her to call back. She gives her direct number. Her voice sounds tight and solemn, her breathing tense and shallow, as if she were trying very hard not to sigh.

_____

Note: ◊ Sigmund Freud, *On Narcissism: An Introduction*, (Karnac Books, 2012) p. 15.

The Drift

The hard drives were returned to her in pieces. The information was still there, she was told, but to see the machinery exposed as it was, the information it contained fragile and vulnerable without its protective shell (which had been removed and was offered up to her separately in two redundant pieces), made her sad and anxious. She needed to tell someone, to offload the frustration and to know she wasn't alone and un-cared-for. She thought of a friend to call. She looked at her phone, the screen open on a photograph. She pressed the back button to return to the main menu – to locate the correct phone number – but it seemed she had navigated too far into the mass of pictures contained by the device. Like a trail of breadcrumbs that did not lead back home, the pictures followed one after another every time she pressed the button. How had she not noticed how far down this rabbit hole she had come? How far away from the point where making contact with her friend was possible?

I would like to thank Rachel Baker, Rebecca Bligh, Rose-Anne Gush, David Panos, Benedict Seymour and Hanna Timonen for supportive, inspiring and productive conversations, and John Kelsey for both such conversations as well as insightful comments on the book itself. I would also want to express my gratitude to Tom Ackers, Antti Kasper, Jenny Nachtigall and Jaakko Pallasvuo, who read drafts of the book and generously applied their critical faculties for its benefit. Many thanks to Inka Achté for the idea for the chapter 'The Challenge' and to Jacob Bard-Rosenberg for posting the Sándor Ferenczi quote used in the chapter, 'The Annals', on his Facebook profile, where I found it. I am ever grateful to Gavin Everall, Lizzie Homersham, Clunie Reid, Jane Rolo and Camilla Wills for the amazing opportunity and collaboration. All the work you have put into this book is much appreciated. Many thanks to Erik Hartin for the design.

The Measure of Reality
Maija Timonen

This publication is part of *G.S.O.H. The Rest is Dark, The Rest is Dark,*
a series of artists' publications commissioned by Book Works from open
submission, and guest edited by Clunie Reid.

Published and Distributed: Book Works
Commissioning Editor: Clunie Reid
Editorial: Gavin Everall, Lizzie Homersham
Proofreading: Jacob Blandy
Design: Erik Hartin
Print: Snel

Printed on Fedrigoni XPer Premium White and Chromolux Metallic Silver.
Typeset using Lineto Brown, Berling Nova Text and Lucida Typewriter.

ISBN 978 1 906012 69 4

Book Works, 19 Holywell Row, London, EC2A 4JB
www.bookworks.org.uk
+44 (0)20 7247 2203

EXCAT

Supported using public funding by
ARTS COUNCIL ENGLAND